Love in a li

Brooke scooted i[n]
of a padded bench seat. Chase ...
her and gave her hand a squeeze. Across from
them, Reverend Bob took his place and pulled
out some papers. Looking around the interior
of the limo, Brooke was overwhelmed by the
garlands of greenery, flowers and ribbons that
decorated the small space.

"Since we have some time before the ceremony,
I'll just point out the special features of this
particular limo." Reverend Bob gestured to the
opaque glass partition behind him. "Soundproof.
We'll lower it during the ceremony so the driver
can be your witness, but once you begin the
honeymoon, it will be raised."

"Honeymoon?" Brooke asked.

"Yes. You've got the limo for two hours." He
gestured for them to move apart, reached
between them and lowered the padded panel.
"You pull that handle there, and the seat will
fold down to make a bed."

Brooke was dumbfounded. He expected...people
actually...

"Cool," Chase said, giving Brooke a wicked grin.

Dear Reader,

I thought I'd get right to the good stuff—aphrodisiacs. After all, this is a Harlequin Temptation, right? In researching the scene where Brooke's sister and Chase's brother are trying to kindle a romance between their siblings, I learned some interesting things. Did you know that through the ages, there were a lot of foods—not just oysters—that were considered to have erotic powers? So, of course, I had to mention them....

One of the aphrodisiacs I used in the book was pine nut soup. Would you believe that pine nuts have been used to inspire romance since 116 B.C.? Do they work? I'll let you be the judge of that. Look below for a recipe.

In the meantime, sit back and have fun watching Chase and Brooke as they struggle to avoid being caught in the romantic snare set for them by their siblings—and find themselves caught up in love anyway!

Have fun,

Heather MacAllister

P.S. You can visit my Web site at HeatherMacAllister.com

Recipe for Pine Nut Soup

Puree $1/2$ cup of pine nuts and 3 egg yolks
in a food processor until you have a smooth paste.
Put the mixture in a saucepan and add 1 cup
of chicken broth and 1 cup of cream. Add $1/8$ teaspoon
of saffron and heat gently, stirring consistently until
the soup thickens. Don't let it boil!
Serve immediately—and enjoy!

PERSONAL RELATIONS
Heather MacAllister

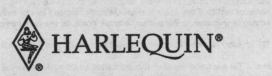

HARLEQUIN®

TORONTO • NEW YORK • LONDON
AMSTERDAM • PARIS • SYDNEY • HAMBURG
STOCKHOLM • ATHENS • TOKYO • MILAN • MADRID
PRAGUE • WARSAW • BUDAPEST • AUCKLAND

To Trudy and Bill Hanes.
And Pilgrim.

ISBN 0-373-25917-4

PERSONAL RELATIONS

Copyright © 2001 by Heather W. MacAllister.

_____Prologue_____

I'm a female West Houston High senior and am looking for a valentine for my overprotective older sister who's cramping my style. She's a babe-in-waiting, not a woofer. If you've got an available older brother who's at least twenty-five, and isn't a troll, call me and let's hook them up. I'll make it worth your while.

"HI, MY NAME IS Jeff Ryan and I'm calling about the ad you put in _Additudes_."

"Oh, yeah. I'm glad my sister didn't answer the phone. Hang on and let me kick my door shut...okay. I'm Courtney Weathers, by the way."

"Uhm, I know who you are—you're in _South Pacific_ at school, right?"

"Yes, just the chorus, but I _am_ the understudy for Nellie."

"Is that good?"

"Well, not as good as being cast as Nellie, since that's the lead, but better than _not_ being the understudy. I mean, people can get colds, right? Anyway, you've got a brother?"

"Yeah."

"Well, is he cute?"

"I'm a guy! I don't know if he's cute or not."

"Do you look like him?"

"Not really. He's my stepbrother, actually, my ex-stepbrother, but he never has a problem getting dates, if that helps."

"So why doesn't he have a girlfriend now? And I'm assuming he doesn't or this call is so over."

"He works all the time and they get mad when he bails on them. And when he's not working, he's bugging me."

"I hear that."

"I mean, he's a great guy, and he's letting me live with him while I finish up at West Houston, but he's got this idea that I'm going to 'follow in his footsteps,' or some garbage like that. He's got my whole life planned out to be just like his."

"Oh, wow! You just described my sister! I've got a major case of goose bumps going here."

"Hey, yeah?"

"I mean, Brooke, that's my sister, she's just so totally into this whole college thing and, like, I'm telling her I want to be an actress and she just *so* won't listen."

"And your parents are listening to her, right?"

"Oh, it's so bad. My dad's working in El Bahar, so they're living overseas and they think that my sister is this perfect goody-goody, mainly because she is. They're always taking her side. It's like they think I'm still this little kid."

"Well...I don't think Chase—my step-bro—is the kind of guy to go for a goody-goody."

"But that's just it—she didn't used to be. It's this responsibility trip she's on. It's got her way too tightly wound. She needs a distraction."

"Yeah...I'm thinking that's what Chase needs. All he does is work—"

"Then is he going to have time to date my sister?"

"If your sister looks anything like you, he'll make time."

"Oh! Hey, thanks. That's sweet."

"Uh, yeah. See, here's the thing. He's trying to set this good example for me and so if he knows I'm watching how he treats your sister, then he won't cancel out, or I'll make a big deal out of it. You know, push the guilt button."

"Okay. So we need to get them together. Do you have anything going on after school?"

"No."

"Why don't you volunteer to help backstage with the sets and props? We need more people."

"I've never done anything like that before."

"They'll teach you and this way, I can introduce Brooke to your brother when they come to pick us up after rehearsal."

"Uhm, I have my own car. Or right now, Chase's."

"Cool. So take it to get the oil changed or something."

"Okay. I'll think of something. So, when do you want to do this?"

"How about tomorrow?"

1

DOWNTOWN TRAFFIC had been worse than usual, so Brooke Weathers was later than she liked to be when she pulled her car into the West Houston High parking lot by the auditorium. Several teenagers gathered in clumps by the brick sign. It looked as though the *South Pacific* rehearsal had already finished.

She scanned the clumps looking for her dark-haired sister and finally found her draped against a silver Porsche as she talked to the occupants.

Some father had just had his midlife crisis, Brooke guessed, since the fancy car was out of the league of most of the students here.

She lowered her window. "Courtney!" she called just as Courtney spotted her. Her sister straightened and gestured for Brooke to come closer.

Talk about lazy. If Courtney could just be bothered to walk a few extra steps, then Brooke could exit now instead of being forced to drive the entire circuit of the parking lot. She shook her head, but Courtney beckoned again.

It had been a long day, a day in which Brooke should have stayed an extra half hour at work and would have, if she hadn't had to pick up Courtney. In spite of the two cars behind her, Brooke shook her head again and gestured back.

Courtney was mad. She stormed over to the car, jerked open the door, then slammed it shut. "Why wouldn't you come over there?"

Brooke got in line for the traffic light. "I didn't feel like driving all the way around the parking lot just because you were in diva mode."

Courtney jammed her shoulder belt into the clasp. "I only wanted you to meet Jeff's brother."

"Who's Jeff?"

"You know, the guy who's working on the sets. That was his brother's car." She gave Brooke a sideways look. "His *single* brother. I told him about you. He acted interested."

"Interested in one thing."

"Oh, come *on* Brooke! Lighten up and maybe you could go out with him."

"Go out with him?" Brooke crossed her fingers in a warding-off-evil-spirits sign. "An older single man with a Porsche? Have I taught you nothing?"

"Yeah, how to spend weekends cleaning the house, then rewarding ourselves with microwave popcorn and a video. Whoopee."

Brooke actually looked forward to Saturday nights with her sister. "You're not dateless *every* Saturday."

"You are," Courtney said quietly.

"I'm too tired to date!" Brooke laughed.

Courtney didn't. "I really wish you'd meet Jeff's brother."

"Thanks, but no thanks."

The *last* thing Brooke needed right now was first-date stress, followed by will-he-call stress, and if he did call, and she did start going out with him, the should-I-or-shouldn't-I stress. With Courtney watching her every move, it was darn well going to be shouldn't. Besides, most men didn't understand why a single woman in her twenties had a self-imposed midnight curfew. But Brooke couldn't apply one set of rules to her dating life and another to Courtney's even though Courtney was still in high school. Brooke shuddered just imagining the arguments. It wasn't worth it.

What would be worth it was the satisfaction she'd feel when she got Courtney into a good college.

Then Brooke could enter the dating scene.

Until then, she didn't need the stress.

"YA GOTTA MEET HER, MAN," Jeff insisted. "If she's anything like Courtney, she's hot."

Chase Davenport gave his brother a long look, then flicked on his turn signal.

"I mean hot in a good way," Jeff tried to explain. "A classy way. Yeah. Classical hot." He dug in his backpack and withdrew a piece of crumpled notebook paper. "Here's her phone number."

"No thanks," Chase said. "I can find my own women."

"For a guy who drives a serious chick magnet like this, you aren't doing such a good job." Jeff picked up Chase's cell phone.

"What are you doing?"

"Programing in Courtney's number in case you change your mind."

Chase didn't bother to object. He could always erase it later. "I was surprised to hear that you were on the stage crew. I didn't know you were interested in that kind of thing." Chase supposed he should be thankful that Jeff was finally showing interest in *something*, but he never would have guessed it would be the school musical.

"Oh, yeah. It's cool."

"Is that how you met Courtney?"

"Everybody knows Courtney," he said.

Chase was beginning to get the picture. Jeff was more interested in this Courtney than he was in the play. He thought back to the girl he'd just met. She was pretty, in a drama student way. She'd had on a bright red sweater and lips to match and long silver earrings that had brushed against her cheeks when she talked. No one could accuse her of being the mousy type, which Chase would have figured more as Jeff's style.

Chase smiled to himself as Jeff went on about lights and computer programs and the sets he was going to help build. This Courtney had high-maintenance written all over her. Jeff might as well learn about high-maintenance women now when he had time for them, because he sure wouldn't have time when he started college in the fall.

And, as Chase had discovered, he wouldn't have time for them when he was trying to establish a career, either.

Chase, himself, didn't even have time for low-maintenance women. But that was all right. Contrary to popular belief, he'd discovered there were actually *no* maintenance women out there—women who agreed that work took precedence for now.

Chase downshifted for the approaching traffic light. The problems started when casual became not-so-casual. That's when the expectations started. And, Chase had to admit, he'd been guilty of changing the terms of a relationship a couple of times, himself. But no more. He had a plan. It was a beautifully simple plan—make a potful of money and semiretire so he could enter the ultimate high-maintenance relationship—a wife and family.

He glanced over at Jeff. They were a lot alike—both children of parents who'd had children before they'd worked through all their selfishness. Jeff's mother still wasn't ready for children, which was why Chase was getting a sneak preview of parenting a teenager. He didn't mind. Jeff was basically a good kid and Chase was flattered that he'd considered fixing him up with Courtney's sister.

But since he suspected high-maintenance ran in the family, he'd have to pass this time.

"JEFF? THIS ISN'T working. It's been days and they won't even wave hello to each other."

"I know. And Chase said he's not going to call your sister."

"It's really too bad, because I think they'd be good together. You know where we went wrong? We shouldn't have tried to set them up. We should have had them accidentally meet somehow."

"Yeah, but they're not going to fall for it now."

"Unless we give them a good enough reason to get together. And we'll have to come up with something soon, because I have to have my film school application and deposit postmarked the day after Valentine's Day."

"What does that have to do with anything?"

"I'll need the money! Brooke won't approve it and without Brooke's okay, my parents won't fork over the cash."

"I still don't—"

"If we come up with something drastic, then film school will look good by comparison, and Chase will be thrilled to let you do what you want to do."

"I don't know what I want to do."

"You'd better decide soon, because you're going to be in a great bargaining position."

"MARRIED? Don't make me laugh." But Brooke didn't feel like laughing. Actually, she felt a little sick and was getting sicker by the moment. Watching her bowl of high-fiber, vitamin-fortified cereal swell into a gray mass as it soaked up the milk didn't help.

"So you'd rather we just live together first?" Courtney smirked. "Mom and Dad will be interested to hear that, especially after their little dairy lecture."

Brooke blinked.

"You know, why would a man buy the cow when

he can get the milk for free?" Courtney took a bite of cereal. Hers still crunched.

"Well, if you want to consider yourself a cow, then I can't stop you," Brooke retorted, goaded by the I've-got-you look on Courtney's face.

"And since I'm eighteen, you can't stop me from getting married, either."

True, true, horribly true. But that didn't mean she wasn't going to try.

Last night was Courtney's third date this week with Jeff Ryan, a boy in every sense of the word. Courtney said he was a fellow senior at West Houston High, but Brooke had a hard time believing it.

Baby fat still padded his muscles and if he had to shave more than once a week, Brooke would be surprised. In fact, when Brooke had met him just last Monday, she'd been surprised that Courtney had been dating him.

He wasn't Courtney's type. Not that there was anything wrong with the boy. If he had another ten years' seasoning, he'd be exactly the type of husband Brooke would want for her younger sister. But right now, he was just potential with hormones and a car.

Yeah, the hormones were there, in spite of the smooth cheeks. Brooke had seen the way he watched Courtney, had seen the way he'd touch her shoulder and arm, and the way he'd tuck her hair behind her ear when they sat next to each other. The car wasn't the only thing with something under the hood.

Brooke studied her sister, realizing she'd taken the wrong tack. She'd been antagonistic and had immediately put Courtney on the defensive. At Courtney's age, she would have hated that. So why couldn't she remember what it felt like to be eighteen, with her whole life ahead of her?

Maybe because she'd never been eighteen with a bright future ahead of her. Maybe because she'd screwed everything up at age seventeen.

Nobody knew better than Brooke how one bad decision could have far-reaching consequences. She was lucky that her parents trusted her enough to keep an eye on Courtney while they worked overseas in El Bahar.

This time, Brooke wasn't going to let them down.

"SHE'S SO CUTE. And you should see the way her eyes crinkle and her nose kind of scrunches up when she laughs."

Chase Davenport threw away the shiny silk tie that exactly matched his shirt and reached for a tie with a raised pattern. One that he could manage to coerce into a knot, which he was finding hard to do when his hands were shaking with suppressed anger. He should have known that Courtney was trouble. "A wife needs a few more qualities than crinkly eyes and a...scrunchy nose." Chase spoke with deceptive mildness, so deceptive that his stepbrother continued to list more of his girlfriend's insipid qualities, oblivious to Chase's disgust.

The boy was barely eighteen and already a gold digger had her hooks in him. Chase had hoped to shield Jeff from women of this type. Women like Jeff's mother.

Of course. Why should Chase be surprised? Jeff no doubt felt comfortable around gold diggers. It ran in his blood. Chase tightened the knot on his tie, satisfied at last. What irony. The son of a gold digger caught by a gold digger.

Too bad it wasn't in Chase to appreciate the irony. He'd long ago abandoned any thoughts of revenge against Zoe Colquitt Ryan Zukerman Brown Davenport el Haibik del Franco. It was his father's business, not his, and Chase had already been out on his own during their brief marriage. Besides, for a while, he'd had a little brother.

Jeff wasn't so little anymore, if he was talking about marriage. It was absurd. He interrupted Jeff's blathering. "Have you actually proposed to the girl?"

"Well, like, yeah. That's how we know we're getting married."

"Did you give her a ring?"

"A ring?"

"An engagement ring, usually a diamond, which you'll slip onto the fourth finger of her left hand. She'll squeal happily, maybe even manage to squeeze out a tear or two, then race over to her girlfriends who will make all kinds of admiring noises while they mentally appraise the size and quality of the stone."

"Uh, I don't think Courtney is that kind of girl."

"They're *all* that kind of girl."

"Courtney's different."

Chase stifled a sigh. "What does her family say?" Maybe they could form an alliance.

"Oh, her sister thinks we definitely should get married."

"Would that be the hot sister?"

"I meant classy." Jeff got that sappy look on his face again. "She can see how much in love we are and said we shouldn't wait too long."

Yeah, sounded like the sister had dollar signs in her eyes, too.

Great. Extricating his stepbrother from this mess was sounding more expensive all the time.

BROOKE DRANK her orange juice as she considered her next remark. "When's the wedding?"

Courtney threw her a startled look, quickly masked. "Well...Valentine's Day is coming up. It would be a shame to miss the opportunity."

Brooke couldn't stand it. This wasn't a moment to be calm after all. "Two weeks? Are you crazy? You're not even out of high school yet. And what about college? You're just going to throw all that away?"

Courtney slammed down her spoon, sending droplets of milk over her sister's sleeve. Brooke dabbed at them, knowing they'd be covered up by her suit jacket.

"Yes, let's talk about college," Courtney said. "I do *not* want to go to Texas, or A&M, or Texas Tech—"

"You don't have to. I've been saving, too, so you can go to a private college if you want. You can go to Baylor, or George—"

"Or the Los Angeles School of Cinematic Arts?"

"No film school."

Courtney sat back and crossed her arms over her chest. "Then I don't see that I'm throwing away much."

"How could you do this to Mom and Dad?"

"Oh, please, not that again."

"Yes, that. They've worked hard so that you—"

"They wouldn't have had to work so hard if it hadn't been for you."

The sisters stared at each other. Brooke couldn't have spoken past the sudden lump in her throat even if she'd wanted to. Courtney suddenly couldn't meet her eyes.

She might have even been going to apologize, except that there was a knock on the kitchen door. Leaping up, Courtney threw open the door to Jeff.

"Jeff," she cooed and draped herself over him. "I've missed you sooo much."

"I've missed you," Jeff said, after he adjusted to Courtney's deadweight and put his arms around her waist.

"I've missed you more."

"I've missed *you* more."

"Missed you more times infinity." Courtney nuzzled against him, her lips inches from his.

Jeff moved even closer. "Missed you more times infinity plus one."

"I missed you—"

"Oh, for God's sake!" Brooke took her bowl of cereal over to the sink and dumped the contents down the disposal. When she glanced over her shoulder she saw that Courtney and Jeff were alternately kissing and murmuring at each other.

Teenagers and their overactive hormones. Why wasn't there a pill for that sort of thing? Surely some doctor somewhere was working on one. Brooke should contribute.

She turned on the disposal, counting on the noise to break the mood.

"Let me put on my lip gloss—it'll just take a sec." Courtney dug the little pot out of her backpack and stepped into the half bathroom off the kitchen.

Good. If she took the time to put on lip gloss, it meant she wasn't planning on a makeout session on the way to school.

"Did Courtney tell you the news?" Jeff stood in the still-open doorway, grinning a little wolfishly in Brooke's opinion. Grinning like a male who'd gotten free milk.

"Yes." Brooke cleared away the rest of the dishes knowing that Courtney would race out of the house without even thinking about it. Another sign of immaturity.

"I was kinda hoping for a congratulations or something."

"Forget it. She's mad. I told you she would be." Courtney dropped the lip gloss into the backpack and slung it over her shoulder.

"How did *your* parents take the news?" Brooke asked Jeff.

"I haven't told them yet," Jeff cheerfully admitted.

Brooke gave Courtney a look. "Before you start griping at me, see what *his* parents have to say."

"My parents aren't together anymore. I live with my stepbrother—well, technically my ex-stepbrother. But he's all for us getting married."

So you'll be out from underfoot. Ex-stepbrother. The poor kid. Outrage mingled with Brooke's frustration. "How old is your stepbrother?"

"Oh, he's old. Thirty or thirty-one. He doesn't like having a party on his birthdays, so it's hard to keep track of them."

Thirtyish? Brooke gritted her teeth. The man should be ashamed of himself. Brooke had visualized someone a couple of years older than Jeff, since any rational adult would have tried to talk him out of marriage.

Therefore, Jeff's stepbrother, or whatever his relationship was, was not a rational adult.

Actually, that wasn't so bad. Brooke could be rational enough for everyone. "Did...did your stepbrother—"

"His name is Chase."

Brooke acknowledged the information with a tight smile. "Did Chase say *when* he thought it was all right for you two to get married?"

"We didn't discuss dates, or anything," Jeff admitted as Courtney nudged him in the ribs.

"He probably didn't realize you wanted to do it before you finished high school. When you stop and think about it, you'll be missing a lot of fun."

"Why would we have to miss anything?" Courtney asked.

"Because...because you'll be too busy for anything but school and work. How do you think you're going to afford an apartment?"

Their arms encircled each other. "We won't have to work," Jeff told her. "Chase said we could live with him. Isn't that cool?"

"Cool" wasn't the word Brooke would have chosen. Idiotic. Irresponsible. Moronic. Those were much better words. They had the added benefit of applying both to the situation and to Jeff's brother.

Brooke was so angry that she found it hard to breathe. She was going to handle this herself. She was not going to bother her parents with it. But she was most definitely going to bother Chase Davenport.

2

"MAN, DID YOU see her face?"

"Oh, yeah. I think just a *little* more and we'll have them."

BY THE TIME she got to work, Brooke was a seething cauldron of rage. What Courtney had actually said was a "seething cauldron of *repressed* rage" but Brooke didn't think her rage was going to be repressed much longer.

The only reason she didn't go directly to Chase Davenport's office after Jeff had helpfully supplied his business card, was that she had three scheduled interviews this morning.

Brooke was a personnel assistant for Haldutton oil. She'd gradually, but doggedly, worked her way up the corporate ladder and now administered screening interviews for clerical job candidates. When she got her degree in a year, she'd be in a strong position for promotion.

Brooke had spent seven years in night school working toward a business degree. She'd desperately wanted to finish before Courtney went off to school, but getting this far was the best she could do. She wanted to set an example for Courtney, to show her how much she valued education. To let Courtney see how hard it was to work and go to school at the same time.

Courtney wasn't going to have to do that. After all, it was Brooke's own fault that she'd had to get her degree the slow way. Courtney shouldn't have to suffer for Brooke's poor judgment.

And now...and now after all the long nights and the hours and hours of study, the sacrifices... Did Courtney think she actually enjoyed being a drudge? If Brooke were feeling really sorry for herself she'd dwell on all the valentineless Valentine's Days she'd had in the past few years.

No, she hadn't had time for a relationship. She'd tried dating a couple of guys, but frankly, they hadn't been worth missing sleep over.

There'd be time next fall, she thought. Next fall when Courtney went off to one of the colleges where Brooke had sent applications. The same ones she'd applied to, but had had to turn down the acceptances.

Damn it, Courtney was *not* going to get married and throw away her future.

SO YOU THINK you can do a better job of raising him than I did you? Chase's father's words whispered through his mind.

Yes, he had thought he could do a better job with Jeff. The boy needed a stable environment. All children needed security, not a father who traveled most of the time and when he *did* come home, would announce that it was time to move again.

Once, Chase and his mother had lived in a hotel room for a month while they waited for their new house to be ready. Two days before they were to move in, his father had laughingly told them they were moving on and wasn't it lucky that they hadn't unpacked yet?

Jeff's mother had been just as bad. So, when Jeff had asked to stay with Chase during high school, Chase had readily agreed.

And now this.

Man, wouldn't his father get a laugh out of it when he heard.

No, Jeff wasn't getting married, at least not any time soon.

Chase reached for his cell phone and looked at the number Jeff had programed in. He supposed nobody was home now, but tonight, he was going to find out how much it would take to buy off Courtney Weathers—and her sister.

BROOKE MANAGED to suppress her anger for the duration of her interviews, although none of the applicants passed her screening. She hoped it wasn't a coincidence.

At ten forty-five, her hand shaking so much she couldn't punch the number on the telephone, Brooke had to shut the door to her tiny office. She started to jog in place, hoping to work off some steam.

Jogging didn't cut it, even after she kicked off her pumps, so Brooke resorted to old-fashioned jumping jacks. The jumping part was fine, but her panty hose gave her trouble during the jack part. She was ready to take them off as well, when a sudden easing in pressure heralded a run in her stockings. At least something could run in this small place.

Bare legs were better than a giant run, so Brooke ripped off her panty hose, tossed them in the wastebasket, did four more jumping jacks and breathlessly punched out Chase Davenport's office number. While the number rang, she looked at the business card. He was a commercial property agent for the MacGinnis Group. In other words, a glorified salesman. A slick, glorified salesman, she added when she remembered the silver Porsche.

Brooke got his voice mail, but didn't want to leave a message and punched zero for assistance.

"Mr. Davenport is at lunch," the receptionist confirmed. "And is scheduled to go directly off-site from there."

"Off-site?" Brooke asked.

"To visit one of our properties."

"Oh. And when do you anticipate his return?"

"May I tell him who is calling?" the receptionist countered, frankly a little late for true professionalism in Brooke's opinion.

"I'm in the Haldutton personnel department. We'd like to check a reference." Brooke's face had heated even before she told the lie. Which wasn't exactly a lie—not much of one, anyway. She was extremely interested in Jeff Ryan's references.

"It's difficult to predict, but you could try back around three-thirty."

Brooke thanked her and hung up before the receptionist could ask for her name again.

Three-thirty. There was no way she could do jumping jacks until three-thirty.

Fortunately, she didn't have to. She even managed to choke down a light carbohydrate-less lunch so her mind would be clear when she went to do battle.

She was calm. She was focused. She was rational.

And then the phone rang.

"Hi, Brooke! Are you busy?" Courtney sounded way too happy.

"What's wrong?"

There was a disgusted sigh. "*Nothing* is wrong. Why do you always think that?"

"Where are you?"

"With Jeff. Rehearsals were canceled while the choir director works with the soloists, so we thought we'd come downtown and go ring shopping! Jeff is getting the money from his brother right now. Want to come?"

Ring! Unfocused, irrational thoughts bombarded her. "I—I have an appointment this afternoon," Brooke said. "In fact, I should be leaving right now."

"Okay!" Courtney said breezily. "Just thought I'd check. You wouldn't want me to settle for a ring that was too small, would you?"

Brooke saw an out. Jeff would probably freak when he saw the price of diamonds. "Oh, most definitely not. After all, you'll be wearing this ring *forever*. It's got to be special. You don't want it to look chintzy."

"Well, no." Courtney sounded uncertain.

"All your friends will see it."

"Yeah, they're gonna be jealous."

"Just remember the four C's."

"What are those?"

"Cut, color, clarity and size."

There was a short silence. "That's only three C's."

"Well, the other one means size."

"Oh. It probably doesn't begin with C because it's the most important."

Brooke was too frazzled to contradict her. "Whatever. Have a good time."

"Okay, bye!"

Brooke gripped the phone and tried to take deep, calming breaths, but only succeeded in making herself light-headed.

Carat. The fourth C was carat. Oh, well, never mind. She'd planted the seeds of greed and it might make Courtney think twice about marriage.

That didn't sound right, but she wasn't going to worry about it now. Grabbing her purse from the bottom file drawer at her desk, she headed for Chase Davenport's office.

"HEY, MAN, like, I need to borrow some major bucks."

Chase winced and tilted back in his chair. "How major?" he asked Jeff, keeping his voice deliberately casual. "Concert ticket major? Car major? Spring break trip major?"

"Engagement ring major. You know, a real diamond."

Ice formed in his veins. "Jeff."

"And I'm not talking about a promise ring here. I want the real thing—like my mother has."

Zoe's diamond size had increased with each marriage. The one she had now could serve as the practice rink for the Olympic ice-skating competition.

"I see." Chase straightened, thinking quickly. "Why don't we talk about this when I get home tonight?"

"'Cause Courtney and I are going ring shopping now. No rehearsal today, so we've got time."

"Jeff—"

"Courtney's asking her sister to come with us to make sure we get a good one. She said something about C's and that size was important."

A red haze crossed Chase's vision. "Make sure you inform Courtney and her sister that any major withdrawals from your trust account must be approved by me."

"Well...like, that's not going to be a problem, is it? I mean, if you've got issues, I can always ask my mom."

Who would see nothing wrong with her son buying a diamond.

Back off, back off. "Hey, it's your money, but I couldn't look your mother in the eye if I let you buy an inferior stone. You know how she is about diamonds. Just don't buy anything without me seeing it first."

"Hey, no prob."

Yes, prob. Big prob.

CHASE DAVENPORT worked in a nice, shiny building several streets over from Brooke's own office building. She was able to reach it through Houston's underground tunnel system, though she had blisters on the backs of her heels by the time she arrived.

As she took the escalator from the tunnel and emerged through the atrium, she was relieved to see that his company, the MacGinnis Group, was, like hers, one of the last bastions of proper business dress, with none of this business casual nonsense. Brooke was very happy to wear a suit, thank-you-very-much. It gave her authority and kept her comfortable in an office that was air-conditioned ten months out of the year.

When she reached the ground floor, she headed for the rest rooms and combed her hair, checked her makeup, and applied the Band-Aids she carried in her wallet to her blisters.

She wanted to look mature—intimidatingly mature, since Chase so clearly wasn't.

The fact that he might not have returned to his office yet didn't occur to her until she was actually asking for him at the reception desk.

"Brooke Weathers," she gave her name to the receptionist, who sat in the center of a round room with hallways leading off it like a spider in the center of her web. "Tell him it's personal."

The receptionist murmured into her headset, then looked at Brooke in pseudo sympathy. "Could you be more specific?"

The nerve of him. There were so many things she

could say—*Sure, tell him I'm from the free clinic. I have the results of his tests and thought he'd like to hear them in person.* Or...*He's behind on his Porsche payments and I'm here to repossess.* Even better, *Tell him the rabbit died.*

Honestly. Anyone who ignored the "personal" label did so at his own risk. However, tempting as it was to be flippant, Brooke merely said, "Tell him I'm Courtney Weathers's sister."

The receptionist was relaying that information when a door off one of the hallways opened.

"I heard."

A man in a crisp long-sleeved shirt rolled to his forearms stood staring at her. Although several dozen yards and a blond receptionist separated them, Brooke felt the tsunami-sized waves of hostility headed her way.

He wasn't the pudgy, balding, affable goof she'd been expecting. Nope. No pudge, no bald spot and an expression of glacial politeness.

He jerked his head to indicate that she should join him in his office, then disappeared inside.

Make that an expression *bordering* on politeness. Brooke hesitated, unwilling to concede a battle so early.

On the other hand, the important thing here was not her pride. Her goal was to keep Courtney from doing something she would surely regret. And that was the only reason Brooke ignored the fact that Chase Davenport had all but told her to heel, and followed him into his office.

WELL, THE SISTER hadn't wasted any time getting over here once she heard Chase had a hold on Jeff's wallet.

Yeah, after Jeff's mother had divorced Chase's father, she'd made a couple of lucky marriages and now had more money than even she knew what to do with. Chase had hoped Jeff hadn't known exactly how much money Chase was managing for him, but someone, probably that flake of a mother of his, must have told him. He'd probably bragged about it at school and the result was this: trouble in a navy blue suit.

She was mad, he could tell that right off. She held her chin up and looked him right in the eye. Ordinarily, he'd like that in a woman, but this sure wasn't ordinary.

And neither was the internal wallop he got once she came close enough for him to see that she was a toned-down version of her sister. The hair wasn't as short, wasn't as black, the lips weren't as red, the body wasn't as thin—and the few pounds had been put to excellent use.

But his response was just the natural response of a male in his prime to an attractive female. It was biological. Nothing to get worked up about.

He deliberately ran his gaze over her, taking in a suit that showed signs of wear and hadn't been all that expensive to begin with. Still she'd made the effort. Too bad the red lines on her feet from her shoes, and the fact that her legs were bare, undermined the professional image she was trying to convey.

Chase made a very comfortable living selling and

managing commercial property, mostly because he was good at judging a potential client's net worth. He'd been wrong a couple of times, but that was when he'd first started out and had been fooled by the "good ole boys" who'd dress down and pepper their speech with double negatives and college football talk. That was when he'd taught himself to notice the details—like the expensive ostrich boots, the custom hat, and the pinkie rings that they wore with the plaid shirts and faded jeans.

It was all in the details—and the details here said gold digger.

He smiled. Piece of cake.

From his power position behind his desk, he watched her cross no-man's-land—the distance between the door and his desk. He didn't bother to stand. He saw her glance at the overstuffed chair with the sprung seat. All but the tallest of men would sit in that chair and discover that they were inches shorter than Chase. She'd probably disappear altogether.

If only it were permanent.

He gave her a once-over. She wasn't all that bad, considering. With the nose and the swingy haircut she was kinda cute.

No, not cute. Cute was appealing and appealing was bad. Not cute.

Cute in this case was being used as a weapon. She probably disarmed all her victims with that cultivated lil'-ole-me cuteness.

Fortunately, he was immune. "What can I do for you?" he asked, feeling his lips curl in a smirk.

"I'm Brooke Weathers," she said and held out her hand, not extending it fully. If he intended to shake her hand, he'd have to rise from his chair.

Very good move on her part. She was clearly no stranger to negotiations and that was important to know.

As Chase decided whether to insult her by ignoring her gesture, their eyes locked. Hers were brown. The thought came out of nowhere. Certainly, he didn't want to notice her eye color. Or the freckles dancing across her nose that made him think of summers spent at the beach in Galveston.

Freckles weren't cute. Freckles were a sign of sun damage, he told himself.

He was going to shake her hand, he decided. There was no advantage to be gained by insulting her. This wasn't about power, this was about getting Jeff out of the mess he was in.

Chase slowly rose to shake her hand. They touched, palms sliding together. Warming. Fusing. So many sharp tingles pricked his hand that he looked down, expecting to see that she had one of those joke buzzers.

No buzzer.

Must be static electricity, but it was giving him one heck of a jolt.

Her hand was cool and trembled slightly. A traitorous part of him noted her nervousness and wanted to reassure her.

"Have a seat," he offered gruffly and resumed his own.

She wasn't falling for that and perched on the padded arm of the chair.

She looked cute.

Maybe thinking of her as cute wasn't a bad thing. He'd outgrown cute. Jeff hadn't, which was why he was in this mess. But Chase wasn't attracted to cute, summer beach bunnies with freckled noses anymore.

Besides, the women he worked with had banished the word "cute" as belittling.

He smiled. "You look cute sitting like that."

"I want to discuss Courtney and Jeff with you," she said as though he hadn't spoken.

Chase leaned back, his body language deliberately insulting. "I thought you might."

It backfired.

She let her gaze drift over his face and sweep across his shoulders, her eyebrows making a subtle not-bad-but-buddy-I've-seen-better quirk upwards.

Chase felt sweat gather in his armpits.

She continued her survey, her gaze bouncing down his ribs. His stomach contracted involuntarily. A smile whispered across her mouth and her gaze rolled south of his belt and stopped.

Stopped.

A drop of sweat trickled down his side. His throat went dry as he battled self-consciousness.

Oh, she was good, he reluctantly conceded, forced to adjust his posture before he embarrassed himself.

As soon as he did so, she gave him a limpid look.

Okay, round two to the sister. "It sure didn't take

you long to get over here after you heard about the ring," he snapped.

"Can you blame me?"

"Someone in your position? Not at all."

"Then you must have known I would disapprove."

"Well, gee. Sometimes our plans just don't work out the way we want them to."

He saw her grit her teeth. "Understand that I want the best for Courtney," she managed to say.

"I'm sure you do." He straightened. "Just how much is that 'best' going to cost?"

She looked momentarily confused. "It depends on which college she attends."

"College. Well, that's a twist I hadn't expected." He glared at her. "I guess this beats filling out all those scholarship forms."

"What are you talking about?" The confusion was back in her eyes. What an actress. Must be where Courtney got it.

"I'm talking about this shakedown."

"Shakedown?"

"Yeah, this great little hustle you've got going here." He opened a drawer, withdrew a leather-covered triplicate checkbook and register. "Tell me— how many other boys' parents have contributed to your sister's...*scholarship* fund?"

She stormed to her feet, the very picture of af-fronted virtuous femininity. "No one has contributed anything!"

"Then they've got stronger nerves than I do. So you've got a break here. How much?"

Her mouth opened and closed. Chase supposed she hadn't been ready for him to capitulate so quickly.

"Are you trying to bribe me into giving my consent to their marriage?" she asked.

"Consent?" He gave a crack of laughter. "Cut the act, sweetheart. I'm offering to buy you off, and you know it." His pen hovered over the checkbook. "Let's see...private school, I don't think so. Courtney looks like a junior college girl to me."

"Wait a minute—"

Chase dropped his smile. "This is a 'take-it-or-leave-it' offer."

"Suppose you explain exactly what I might be taking or leaving."

He finished scrawling on the check, ripped it out and tossed it across the desk. "You and your sister take your hooks out of Jeff and throw him back into the pond. There are bigger fish out there."

"I suppose that's your clumsy way of saying that you *don't* want Jeff to marry my sister and it's worth—" She picked up the check and stared incredulously. "Ten thousand dollars? Are you kidding?"

"More money than you've ever seen in one place, right sweetheart?"

"Oh, please. This is your brother—"

"Stepbrother. And a former one at that."

"Still—shouldn't there be another zero?"

"That's all you're getting."

She tossed the check back at him. "This may be all Jeff's future is worth to you, but I'll have you know that my sister is worth a heck of a lot more than ten grand. Besides, I'm really concerned about how out of date you are with college tuition costs."

"News flash—that sister of yours isn't exactly baccalaureate material. The only degree she's after is her MRS."

"What time warp did you beam through? Comments like that are politically incorrect now."

He gazed up at her. "Actually, I was paying her a compliment. What I felt like saying was that your sister has mistress written all over her. She's going to be some rich, old man's plaything. At best, she'll be a trophy wife."

BROOKE'S KNEES gave out and she sank deep into the chair.

Who did he think he was? More importantly, who did he think *she* was?

He leaned forward and slid the check toward her. "Your sister's not bad looking. Use this and fix her up a little. Buy her some nice clothes, a good haircut, maybe a nose job—but get her the hell away from my stepbrother."

A hot fury burned away the desensitizing layers of composure Brooke had grafted onto her emotions. It had the effect of exposing all her feelings to an intensity she hadn't experienced for years.

Everything was...more. The afternoon sun coming through the window was brighter. The air from the heating vent was dryer, the breath mint she'd eaten before coming in here was mintier.

Chase's shirt was crisper, his jaw sharper, his eyes colder.

And the dimple in his chin was deeper.

It looked old-fashioned—kind of forties Hollywood. She hadn't noticed many men with clefts in their chins these days.

But this wasn't about the cleft in his chin, or his jaw, either, or her pride. This was about...about...

Yes, it was, too, about pride, damn it!

He, this jerk, this old-fashioned male chauvinist *pig*, thought that Courtney wasn't good enough for his brother. He didn't care that two young people were making a major life decision based on their hormones. His only objection was that Courtney wasn't *good* enough or classy enough for his—for Jeff.

Brooke was furious and it hurt to breathe. She couldn't draw enough air into her lungs anyway.

"Courtney is worth ten of Jeff! Marriage to her would be the best thing that could happen to him. He might even grow up."

Slowly, Chase rose and leaned over the desk, propping himself on his fists. "He doesn't need to grow up that way. Right now, he's still young enough to believe in hearts and flowers and getting tickets to the prom. He doesn't need to know that there are women out there only interested in him for his money."

"What money? He had to borrow a few dollars from Courtney to pay for pizza the other night. I know, because she had to borrow the money from me."

"I'm not talking chump change, and you know it."

Actually, pizza was more than chump change to someone who was watching every penny. That had blown Brooke's lunch budget and she'd had to brown bag it twice to get back on track.

"You've seen the kind of car Jeff drives," he continued.

"The ten-year-old Honda?"

Chase flushed. "That's my car. It runs great. Jeff's is the silver Porsche. His mother gave it to him."

"Then what are you doing driving it?"

"His grades weren't up to par the past six weeks and that's the deal. He maintains a B average, or we switch cars."

"Oh." What a great incentive. How could this jerk have thought of it?

Unless he *wanted* Jeff to blow off his grades so he could drive the Porsche. But as much as she wanted to believe that, especially after his next comment, she didn't.

He eyed her. "You're not trying to tell me you didn't know he's sitting on a nice little trust fund."

"Not until you just told me. And it wouldn't have mattered anyway."

"Tell me another one."

"Jeff doesn't look like a trust fund kid."

"He hasn't been one for all that long," Chase grudgingly conceded.

Their eyes met. Brooke's anger had unaccountably cooled and as it did so, she found herself replaying their argument. He must have been doing the same because at that moment, his eyebrows drew together and he echoed her thoughts. "Let me get this straight—you're *against* them getting married?"

"If it means Courtney giving up college, you better believe it."

"Oh." He straightened, his forehead still creased as he looked down at her. "Then that means—"

"We're on the same side," Brooke finished.

3

"JEFF! BROOKE'S OFFICE said she's on her way over to see Chase!"

"Is that good?"

"Are you kidding? Film school, here I come!"

BROOKE AND CHASE stared at each other, each absorbing the implications of their changed status. Then they let out twin sighs of relief.

For the moment, all Brooke could think about was that she only had half the battle to fight she had before.

And then a wide grin split Chase's face, which pretty much changed him from a shoo-in for jerk of the century—to...something else.

He dropped his head and shook it slightly, then looked skyward before beaming that smile her way again.

Brooke felt its impact like a punch to her stomach. She was still in the process of realigning her opinion of him and didn't have any attractive-man filters in place.

Oh, boy.

Trying to regroup, she blurted out, "But if you're against them marrying—and I'm including any living-together arrangement—then why did you tell them they could live with you?"

"I never—oh, yeah." He winced. "Jeff had asked me to help him find a job so he could support the little gold—" Chase broke off abruptly. "No offense."

"None taken." Which wasn't strictly true, but she was feeling generous. Relief could do that to a person.

"He wanted a job right away so he could earn the apartment deposit. I want him concentrating on his grades, not staying up half the night bagging groceries, so I said they could live with me."

Brooke nodded. "I probably would have said the same thing."

He turned down the wattage on his smile. "So what was with the get-a-big-diamond advice?"

It was Brooke's turn to look sheepish. "I hoped that Jeff would be shocked at how much they cost. I thought maybe it might start an argument—or at least a discussion. Money is the number one topic couples argue about. I was just buying time until I could talk with you."

The warmth was back in his expression. Unfortunately, she was feeling a little—okay, a lot of—warmth of her own.

He drew a deep breath. "This calls for a drink. And I'm talking *all* the caffeine and sugar. The full monty."

He came from behind the desk and headed toward a worktable that had a wooden file cabinet beneath it.

Except as she quickly saw, it wasn't a file cabinet but a small refrigerator filled with cans and bottles.

"Ohh..." She closed her eyes. "You wouldn't happen to have a Dr Pepper in there, would you?"

"A woman after my own heart."

Or maybe not. There was an awkward silence during which Chase sorted through the selections in the little refrigerator and they ignored any inflammatory interpretations of what he'd said.

"The vending machines on this floor only carry Coke, so I've got my own private stash." He squatted down and dug way in the back, past bottles of water and diet sodas until he pulled out a single can of Dr Pepper.

"Here it is." He held out the can as though it were a bottle of vintage burgundy.

Brooke's mouth watered in anticipation. "You only have one?"

"Yeah. It's for emergencies. We'll have to split it." He reached for two glasses emblazoned with a gold "$10,000,000 Seller" emblem, and removed the ice tray from the tiny freezer compartment.

"Oh, I couldn't...you take it. I'll have a can of whatever else you've got in there."

"No way. We both deserve it." He popped the top and Brooke heard a fizz as the liquid was poured over ice. "It's been one of those days."

Gesturing for her to take one of the two club swivel chairs on her right, he pulled one away from the worktable with his foot and handed her the drink.

"To our new alliance." Chase clinked his glass to hers, then downed half the drink in a single swallow. "Oh, that hit the spot."

"You can say that again." Brooke closed her eyes and felt the sugar and caffeine jack up her pulse. Sure she'd pay with a sugar low later, but right now, she didn't care.

"So...Brooke is it?"

She nodded.

"I'm really sorry for—"

Brooke stopped him by vigorously waving her hands. "No—please. Let's just start over."

He grinned. "I like your style."

Brooke hadn't been conscious of having a style. She'd just wanted to put the whole ugly confrontation behind them.

"So what do you do, Brooke?" Chase eased back in the chair, probably unaware that his shirt was stretched across his chest in a way that...in a way she normally didn't notice on a man.

In a way she definitely shouldn't be noticing on Chase. But...well, she did. She was a woman, even though she hadn't been acting like one for the past several years, and he was...waiting for an answer to his question. "I work for Haldutton in the personnel department."

"On Travis, or are you at The Woodlands location?"

"Travis."

"The Travis building is one of the properties we manage."

He gulped more of his drink, making Brooke feel guilty that she'd taken half of it. But this was like smoking the peace pipe after treaty negotiations with the enemy. It would have been rude to refuse the gesture.

"I cannot tell you how relieved I am that we're on the same page here." He slid a sideways glance at her. "We *are* aren't we?"

"If you're on the they'd-better-get-their-education-first page, then we are."

"I am. Just verifying." He set his glass on the laminated tabletop. "Jeff is living with me until he finishes high school. He's a senior now and doesn't know what he wants to do with himself. Which doesn't particularly matter since *I* know what he should do."

To an outsider, that should have sounded unbelievably arrogant, but Brooke not only understood, she felt exactly the same way about Courtney.

"I've spent months going through the college admissions drill with him and when he started talking marriage—*marriage*—I panicked," Chase admitted with disarming candor.

"So did I." A soul mate. The man was her soul mate. He was going through the same thing with his stepbrother that she was going through with Courtney. He *knew*.

"I mean, I pulled some serious strings to get him into Baylor. It's a good, steady school. Not a party school. Jeff doesn't need an excuse to party."

"Oh, I know. I feel the same way about Courtney." The words babbled out. She hadn't met anyone else responsible for a sibling—like a parent, but not a parent—and being able to talk with him was such a *relief*.

"The thing is, I've been so frustrated because she wouldn't fill out the applications. *I* had to do it."

"I know! What is up with that?"

"Well, Courtney claims she doesn't want to go to college. She says she wants to be an actress and being in this play at school has only made it worse. It's not as if I'm telling her she *can't* be an actress, I just want her to be able to support herself and for that, she's *got* to get an education."

"Exactly!" His look of approval made her feel better than it should have.

A lot better. A dangerous kind of better. "So... where did this marriage talk come from? I mean, I thought Courtney and I had a good relationship, but this came out of nowhere."

"Beats me. With a mother like the one Jeff's got, you'd think he'd never want to get married. She's bounced around the world leaving a trail of husbands in her wake—including my father. She dragged Jeff with her, but when he was ready to start high school, he wanted to stay in one place. When he asked if he could live with me, I was more than happy to have him. Our family moved a lot when I was growing up. I didn't have any brothers and sisters and it was hell trying to fit in all the time." He smiled slightly. "Jeff was the only brother I ever had and he's basically a good kid. He just needs some grounding." He looked at her. "Nothing against your sister, but he doesn't need marriage right now."

"Neither does Courtney. And it doesn't make sense for her to want to get married unless..."

"Jeff said she wasn't pregnant."

"No, not that." And Courtney had been mad when Brooke had asked. "But maybe she knows that Jeff has money and figures he'll support her while she's trying to break into acting." Except that Jeff seemed more like the supportee than the supporter. In deference to her new alliance with Chase, Brooke decided not to point that out.

"Don't worry. I'll set them both straight on that. What do your parents have to say about all this?"

"They don't know and I'd rather not tell them if I can avoid it. They're living in El Bahar where my dad is working, so Courtney and I are living in the house while she finishes high school. Technically, I'm her guardian—or I was until she turned eighteen. And by the way, whoever made the stupid law about eighteen-year-olds being legal adults has obviously never been responsible for a teenager."

"I hear you." Chase laughed. "But I've got to tell you, you don't look much older than high school age, yourself."

"I'm twenty-five."

He swept his gaze over her, the sort of gaze that made a woman hold in her stomach. He probably wasn't even aware that he'd done so, but Brooke was. Extremely aware.

And she'd sucked in her stomach.

"Wasn't that kind of a drag to have your sister dumped on you?"

Brooke was shaking her head even before he finished. "No, in fact I was glad." She looked at him, at the face that was considerably friendlier than when she'd first entered the office, at the one person who understood exactly what her responsibilities had been the past several years.

And found herself telling him everything—everything about the day that had changed her life. "When I was her age, I really screwed up. This is a chance to redeem myself."

"What happened?"

"Oh...poor choices and peer pressure. It was spring break my senior year and a bunch of us had gone to the beach at Galveston. I was driving my parents' van. You know that cars are banned from the beach, and there was nowhere to park. Anywhere. The place was packed."

Chase nodded. "I've done spring break in Galveston."

"So you know how it is. Anyway, we finally went out to the tip of the island by some beach houses and just drove on past them onto the beach. We figured if anybody said anything to us, we could tell them we'd rented one of the houses. We had a great time, but a police cruiser caught us sneaking back onto the road that night. I was going to pull over but this guy I liked was with us and he kept telling me to keep driving."

"You tried to outrun a police car?"

"It wasn't like it was a high-speed chase or anything. We were dodging them between the houses. Everybody said I should kill the lights and just pull into one of the driveways until the police car left. So, I turned off the lights and..."

She could still hear Jason's voice laughing and saying, "Way to go, Brooke!" and flinging his arm around her. She still remembered the tight curl of awareness that took over her insides and made her want to do anything to keep it there.

The rest of her friends started chanting, "Go, Brooke! Go, Brooke!"

She'd had a reputation as a goody-two-shoes, which was why *her* parents had let her drive in the first place. All her life she'd followed the rules and this one time when she hadn't...

"I skidded in the sand, missed the driveway and hit the support beam of a beach house."

"Were you all right?" Chase asked immediately.

"Oh, yeah. The airbags went off. The kids in the back weren't wearing seat belts and got thrown forward. Still, we were all lucky—just bruised mostly." She sighed. "The van was totaled, the beach house might as well have been. I think the repairs cost more than building it from scratch would have. Oh, and did I mention that the house was owned by a lawyer?"

"Ouch." He gave her a sympathetic look.

"Yeah. I was completely at fault, we were sued, and there went my college fund, my parents' savings, retirement, the whole bit."

"And you've been beating yourself up about it ever since, right? You look the type."

Brooke gave him a wry smile. Just a little while ago, her type had been compared to a madam in a brothel. "I made a mistake...a really stupid mistake. And I paid for it. I'm still paying for it, I suppose, but Courtney shouldn't have to. My father took the job overseas because of the money he could make and because I told my parents I'd look after Courtney. They trusted me when they didn't have to and I will do anything not to let them down again. So, Courtney is not getting married before she graduates from high school, and she is not blowing off college, either. That's all there is to it."

"Hey." He reached out and covered the hand she'd fisted in her lap.

She watched as his fingers closed around hers in slow motion. She could feel every line in his palm. Warmth enveloped her hand and her wrist. It was well on the way to her elbow before he squeezed gently and released her hand.

"You aren't in this alone anymore," he said quietly, but with an underlying strength that made Brooke want to melt against him and let him carry all the problems on his substantial shoulders.

As she gazed into his dark eyes, Brooke realized that the melting part was still a distinct possibility.

How had she missed the fact that Jeff's ex-relative was a total babe? Of course, his babeness had been hidden when he was in jerk mode and was now brilliantly illuminated by relief and the effects of sugar and caffeine.

She sighed, and the corner of his mouth rose.

"I feel the same way."

Brooke doubted it, she really doubted it.

"So what now?" he asked.

"Now?"

"Jeff and Courtney—how do we cool their jets?"

"Not by telling them they can't see each other."

"You got that right." Chase stood and cleared away her empty glass and his own, then snagged paper and pens from the desk and brought them back with him. "We have to be smart about this—use our heads, not react emotionally."

"Right. Heads, not hormones."

"Exactly."

When he sat, he pulled the chair closer to hers so he could write at the table.

Heads, not hormones. Heads, not hormones.

Hormones were tricky little devils. Up until now, Brooke had simply had to put them in deep-freeze storage until it was safe to thaw them out. Actually, she was looking forward to the thawing—after Courtney left for school.

As Brooke picked up her pen, she couldn't help noticing that Chase's knee was a fraction of an inch away from her own. It was close enough that she could feel the heat from his leg. Heat. She swallowed. Heat could be bad.

"We need a plan." He flashed her a grin. "Preferably the same one."

"Yes, a plan," she echoed brilliantly. But really, how was she supposed to think with him sitting so close and acting like a take-charge male?

She hadn't even known she liked a take-charge kind of guy. She'd always thought there wasn't a lot of difference between the take-charge type and a bully. "So have you got any ideas?" she asked hoping that he wouldn't notice that she'd been staring at him.

"Bribery?"

"Chase, your brother drives a Porsche. What's left for you to bribe him with?"

"Good point." He starting tracing circles—perfect circles—on the paper.

Brooke watched his fingers and the way they held the brushed silver pen. He had nice hands. Nice fingers. Fingers that kept going around and around and around....

She gripped her own pen. Hard. "You know," she said, her voice too breathy, "We could take the opposite tack—throw them together as much as possible and hope they get sick of each other. Or start bombarding them with all the information they'll need to set up house together."

Chase began writing and she watched as the words flowed from his pen. She swayed toward him on the off chance that his elbow might accidentally brush against her.

When she realized what she was doing, she swayed back. "Or even better, we can take them apartment hunting and show them just what a one-bedroom unit in their price range looks like," she added just so she could see him write more.

"Sounds good." He hadn't seemed to notice anything weird about her behavior. "Although, there's a risk that Jeff and Courtney will be too busy being in love to notice the dumps we're showing them."

"There is that."

He gestured to her paper with his pen. "Shouldn't you be taking notes?"

"Oh! Yeah, I guess so." Brooke started writing and belatedly noticed the ink all over her fingers.

Chase exhaled in disgust. "I'm sorry. I shouldn't keep using those cheap giveaway pens. Let me get some paper towels." He disappeared out his office door.

Brooke closed her eyes as the warmth temporarily left her.

What was going on? It was like he had magnets under his skin, or the air around him was ionized or something. Definitely something. Her initial relief at finding that they were on the same side had faded, but her awareness of him hadn't.

It made no sense. She didn't react like this to men, and hadn't flirted with boys even when she'd been a teenager. Slow and cautious, that was her motto—except for that one hideous spring day when she'd "loosened up."

She couldn't afford to be loose, that's all there was to it. She needed to think with her head.

In fact, her head was telling her now that after confessing her reasons for wanting Courtney to have the opportunities she hadn't, she'd bonded with Chase the way patients sometimes bond with their therapists. In either case, it might be understandable, but wasn't appropriate.

So why were her emotions emoting without permission?

Her head hadn't even established whether he was single yet.

So hurry up and figure it out, already!

Suspecting an imminent emotional mutiny, Brooke looked around his office, checking for pictures on his desk or the shelves behind it. Looking for one of him with a woman but there weren't any pictures at all, unless the framed pen-and-watercolor prints of buildings counted.

Chase pushed through the door, paper towels in hand. "Here, let's get you cleaned up." He sat, and instead of handing her the folded square of damp paper towel, he reached for her hand and scrubbed at the ink.

And she let him. She wasn't about to tell him she could do that herself.

His fingers felt strong against hers and the warmth from the hand that held her wrist spread up her arm.

His head was bent toward hers as he tried to rub away the ink. If she stretched her neck just the slightest bit and tilted her chin, his hair might brush against it. The nerves in her neck and chin tingled in readiness.

HE COULD SMELL the remnants of the perfume she'd applied that morning. It was a sexy smell, the musky base that held the scent to the skin. It was also an intimate smell, one he looked forward to after spending long hours in a woman's company and then only when his nose was inches away from the curve of her neck—the way it was close to Brooke's now.

Aside from the big three, two of which could be technically counted as one, the curve of a woman's neck was Chase's favorite part of the female anatomy. He liked it when the traces of perfume mingled with a woman's own unique scent and the way goose bumps rose on her skin when he exhaled softly. He adored soft murmurs that made vibrations against his mouth. Yeah, necks were where it was at.

But that didn't mean he had a fetish about necks in general. Usually, they were attached to a woman he had feelings for.

He had feelings for this woman, all right, but until recently, they'd been antagonistic feelings. They were not get-close-and-naked feelings. Or they shouldn't be.

When she'd told him about her senior year, he'd felt an admiration that she was taking responsibility for her actions. Hardly anyone did these days and he liked her for that. He liked it a lot—that wasn't surprising. What *was* surprising, was that he'd found her determination incredibly sexy. Responsibility was sexy? Who knew?

Not Chase, who'd responded by using the flimsiest of excuses to touch her. Instead of sending her off to the ladies' room to wash her hands, he was scrubbing at stubborn ballpoint pen ink on her fingers and leaning way too close in the process.

She didn't seem to notice, and he should thank his lucky stars that seemed to be the case. Glancing up, he inhaled just the slightest bit, swallowed and forced himself to lean back.

"There," he said, though a slight blue tinge still shadowed the creases in her knuckles. He'd wandered into dangerous territory and the internal red alert signals he'd been ignoring were telling him it was time to wander back.

Brooke slowly withdrew her hand, sensitizing every nerve in his palm as she did so.

Okay, okay. He needed some air and some space and some more air before he did something incredibly stupid. He stood and walked over to his desk to throw away the damp paper towels, taking a few extra moments ostensibly to remove ink smudges from his own fingers.

Jeff, he reminded himself. Think of Jeff.

Jeff was in a potential mess because he was letting his hormones rule his life. He wasn't thinking. Nothing good ever came from letting hormones have their way.

Chase didn't need to look further than his own father for an example. He'd been blinded by Jeff's pretty young mother just months after Chase's own mother had died.

No one said handling passion was easy. After all, the reproductive urge was second only to the survival instinct. Man was programed to be at the mercy of his hormones, but wasn't he given a mind to decide when and where to act on them?

A movement in his peripheral vision caught Chase's attention. Brooke had slipped the heel of her shoe off and was rubbing at a red area around a bandage on the back. It was a private moment and she didn't know she was being observed. Something about the curve of her calf and the sensual rhythm in the way she rubbed the sore spot, the inching upward of her skirt, the flash of thigh...

Chase felt a tightening below his belt and turned away. Not easy, but doable.

This was Jeff's problem. He wasn't turning away. Jeff wasn't using his mind. He was just feeling, caught up in the rush of pleasure at the touch of a woman, the feel of soft curves pressed against him, the anticipation, the feel of bare skin on bare skin....

Okay, Chase wasn't going to think about Jeff anymore. He was going to think about himself, about his goals, his life plan. Sure that plan included marriage and children. And when he was a father, he was damn well going to be around for his kids while they grew up. That's why he was working hard now, because he intended to back off later. Raising kids right took time and his experience with Jeff had only underscored his determination. He was thirty-one, and within another couple of years, he planned to start looking for a wife. When he did so, he was going to use a combination of chemistry *and* logic.

He tossed the damp wad of paper towels in the wastebasket, still surprised that he was experiencing a blast of hormones at his age.

Actually, it had added a pleasant zing to the afternoon, but now his mind was firmly in control once again.

4

"UHM, SO NOW WHAT DO WE DO?"

"Jeff, Jeff, Jeff. You are *such* an amateur. Now, we give them the opportunity to bribe us."

"I BELIEVE that if we work together on this, we'll have a greater chance of making those two see reason."

"Oh, most definitely." Brooke had been reading over Chase's shoulder—his nicely muscled shoulder—as he finished making notes. As he'd said, there was no need for them both to write when there was a photocopy machine just down the hall.

It also allowed Brooke a perfectly legitimate excuse to sit closer to him—as opposed to the illegitimate excuse of brushing imaginary paper towel remnants off his knee, which she'd done earlier.

The memory of hard, warm, muscles beneath worsted wool was prompting her to try to think of something she could brush off his shoulder. Then he flashed that smile of his her way and she forgot all about shoulders and started thinking about lips.

Lips touching, say, other lips. Hers for instance.

"Brooke?"

Had he said something? His lips hadn't been moving had they? "Hmm?"

"You need to move your chair a couple of inches. The leg is blocking my chair."

"Oh." She rolled her chair back. Caught sitting too close and she wasn't even embarrassed. What did that say about her?

She didn't know and had given up trying to understand why she was acting the way she was. For now, she was going with the flow. Something about Chase Davenport appealed to a corresponding something within her. And really, what harm was there in fantasizing about him? It wasn't as though he could read her lust-soaked mind.

As he moved his chair back, Chase scanned the notes they'd spent the past half hour brainstorming. "Looking at everything we're going to have to do to get those kids back on track makes me glad I'm past that age where I was at the mercy of my hormones."

"Oh, yes. Definitely." Although Brooke wasn't so certain she was past that stage yet.

On second thought, sure she was. She'd just been indulging herself and now it was going to have to stop. She stood—and wobbled.

"Steady there." He'd thrust out his arm as she'd grabbed his shoulder. His hand settled at the curve of her waist alerting all the nerves in the vicinity.

Brooke looked down at him. "I guess I've been sitting too long."

He didn't move his hand and she didn't release his shoulder.

Several heartbeats throbbed by. She saw banked awareness in his expression and knew he saw the same in hers, although she wasn't doing a very good job of banking anything. Her skin felt hot. Her eyes were probably glowing.

But this was ridiculous. She was projecting something she wanted to see.

With great reluctance, she drew her hand away from his shoulder.

At the same time, he slid his hand away from her waist, brushing it over her hip—which could have been because she'd turned slightly at the last minute in an act of utter shamelessness.

She should leave. Now, while she could. "I should leave. Now."

"I'll make your copy." He stood too quickly—too quickly for her to move back and give him enough space.

He jostled against her, which necessitated another round of shoulder grabbing and waist supporting.

"Sorry."

"My fault."

And their eyes met again.

Chase seemed to give himself a mental shake and pointed toward the door. "The copy machine...it'll only take a sec." He edged away from her as he spoke.

"I could come with you and just leave from there."

"No!" He quickly composed his features. "What I mean is, the room is small." He was at the door. "Really just a closet . . ."

He almost ran from the office.

The man was clearly rattled. She hadn't imagined it.

Brooke closed her eyes as a hot blush started at her chest and flamed over her neck and cheeks. How was she going to face him again after her behavior? He'd figured out that she had the hots for him and it had made him uncomfortable.

She was trying to decide whether or not she should say something—and what—when Chase returned, his breath coming quickly.

"Here's your...here it is." He held out her copy.

Professionally, that's how she'd behave. Retrieving her purse, she hooked it over her shoulder and reached for the paper. "Thank you."

Her fingers tugged at the paper.

Chase held on and she looked at him questioningly.

"Brooke..."

Oh, no. "I appreciate this..." She tugged harder. "...so..."

"Brooke."

"...much!" She yanked the paper out of his grasp. The momentum propelled her backwards.

He reached for her.

"I'm okay!" They both looked at the trembling paper in her hands. Brooke pretended that she was in the process of folding it prior to putting it in her purse.

"You're not okay."

"I said I was okay, so I'm okay. Okay?" Brooke

gave up on folding and jammed the paper in her purse, then discovered she couldn't work the clasp.

"Well, I'm not."

"You're not what?"

"I'm not okay." He took a step toward her. "There's something going on here."

"Nothing's going on!" Brooke gave up on the clasp and hooked the strap over her shoulder.

"Sure there is. I felt it and I know you felt it, too."

"What I felt was relief." Brooke took a step toward the door. Chase mirrored it. "And gratitude," she answered with another step. "I'm pretty sure gratitude was in there, too."

His voice dropped to a husky murmur. "I'm not feeling any gratitude at all."

How had he managed to come closer without her noticing? Brooke edged back. Her hands weren't the only parts of her that were shaking. There was a whole war going on inside her. Head and hormones were battling it out. *Touch him! No, run! Stand still! Escape!*

"And I'm definitely not relieved."

"Oh, that." She giggled—*giggled*. "That would be the leftover adrenaline from being so angry earlier. There wasn't a big enough blowup to use it up. We just...kind of fizzled."

"The word you're looking for is sizzled."

"No, no, I'm pretty sure it's f-fizzled."

Brooke felt the corner of his desk against her thigh and realized that she had been edging backward in a circle and the door was on the other side of the room.

"Or in my case, frazzled." She tried to slide along the edge, but Chase clamped a hand down on the desk. He was close. So very close.

"When I'm frazzled, I act ditsy sometimes. And I'm not ditsy."

Brooke moved the other way and met his remaining hand. She was now caged by his arms. Oh, boy. "Chase?"

"We need to talk."

Talking was bad. Very bad. Brooke swallowed. "Please don't talk."

Chase gave her a predatory smile like no other she'd ever seen. "Works for me." With that, he swooped his mouth down on hers.

Acting instinctively, Brooke more than met him halfway. There was an unfortunate cracking of teeth against teeth before Chase ordered gruffly, "Hold still," and kissed her again.

It was a full-court-press kiss. A hit-one-out-of-the-park kiss. A ninety-nine-yard return kiss. And Brooke wasn't even a sports fan. But she didn't have to be to recognize a winning kiss when she experienced one.

This kiss was a toe curler.

She sighed into it, looping her arms around Chase's waist. Apparently his admonishment to "hold still" didn't extend to her tongue, which he'd invited to a pretty torrid tango.

And Brooke tangoed. It was sweet and sexy and hot. She even let him lead—part of the time.

Everything was happening fast, yet not fast enough.

Everything was happening with the force of an explosion, yet she wanted more.

With one kiss, Chase had mowed down every mental objection Brooke had to getting involved too quickly. Her whole dating timeline for physical intimacy was shot to pieces in one fell swoop. She'd stopped thinking rationally and was able to communicate with herself in nothing but clichés.

Clichés were trite and totally inadequate for the task of explaining what was going on with Chase. So Brooke no longer bothered. Did she care what she thought of herself? Not at the moment. Was she going to stop?

Not while she could still breathe.

Sometime during the moments Brooke had wasted arguing with herself, Chase had drawn his arms around her and was clutching her to him as though he thought she might escape. Silly man. She had no intention of going anywhere, or at least not until her lips gave out.

Purely to reassure him, she pulled him closer to her, then reached down and squeezed a nicely muscled butt.

Chase jerked his mouth away from hers. No! That wasn't the idea at all.

They both stared at each other, dragging in breaths as though they'd just finished the two-hundred meter Olympic trials.

"You...stopped!" Brooke accused him.

"I paused." He reached behind her and shoved. Brooke heard papers and files slither to the floor, followed by the shattering crash of a coffee mug filled with pens.

Chase's strong hands gripped her waist as he hoisted her onto the desk and stepped between her legs. "Better?"

"Closer is always better."

Instead of kissing her again right away, Chase dropped his mouth to the side of her neck and inhaled deeply, then cupped her face and gazed into her eyes.

In that moment, he personalized everything. He wasn't just kissing—he was kissing *her*—and he was making sure she knew it.

It was the extra touches like those that separated the gifted lovers from the technically accomplished. The fact that Chase was both had pretty much turned Brooke's insides to jelly.

She shivered, her breathing shaky. A slow smile—the only slow thing so far—pulled at the corners of his mouth. His thumbs softly brushed across her cheeks and down her jaw. He pressed a kiss against her temple which pretty much did it for Brooke. She was his from that moment—whenever, wherever, however.

Still cradling her jaw, Chase deliberately brought his mouth down on hers tilting until the fit was exquisitely perfect. With a murmur of satisfaction, he drew her into an increasing whirl of sensation.

Brooke stopped thinking—not that she'd been doing all that much—and just felt.

What she felt were Chase's hands roving over her back, heating her skin even through her jacket, and the play of muscles in his back as she did a little roving of her own.

Inhaling sharply, Chase parted the lapels of her jacket and scooped it off her shoulders. Brooke wiggled her arms out and flung the jacket off to the side.

Ah, that was better. For now.

Now didn't last very long. Brooke felt Chase's fingers tugging the proper white shell out of the waistband of her skirt and then his hands spanned across the bare skin of her back.

Skin! What a good idea. Why hadn't she thought of that before? Kissing him even more deeply, Brooke tugged his shirt out of his slacks and started unbuttoning. The buttons weren't cooperating and she made a little sound of frustration.

There was an answering sound from Chase that vibrated along her tongue. It felt so good, she momentarily stopped to savor the sensation.

Chase moved his hands to help her and she batted them away.

The next thing she felt was the clasp of her bra giving way.

"No fair," she murmured, finally breaking the kiss to see what she was doing.

"We'll have to do something about that."

She worked loose two more buttons before Chase covered her breasts with his palms.

Her breath caught between her teeth. "Okay, fair enough!"

"I can be a lot more fair than this."

"But I can't touch you the way I—"

In a breathtakingly quick movement, Chase ripped his still-partially buttoned shirt over his head and reached for her. Brooke pressed her lips against the warm skin and felt the pounding of his heart against her mouth.

She'd never been this aroused in her life. She was crazy with it, wanton with it. She was in complete hormonal meltdown. Chase's hands skimmed up her ribs and she raised her arms so her shell and bra could ease over her head, then she clutched him to her.

As his mouth closed over her breast, a primitive cry echoed in the office.

She'd made that noise. Brooke buried her mouth against his shoulder to muffle any more outbursts and surrendered to the delicious sensations.

Chase stroked her thighs and eased her skirt up to her hips, Brooke rocking from side to side to help.

The rocking felt so good, she continued as Chase's fingers fluttered and teased the inner skin of her thighs.

Every once in a while, she gave his shoulder a little nip of encouragement. She couldn't help it, but the last little nip must have not been so little because Chase gasped, then reached under her skirt to drag her panties down her legs.

Brooke leaned back on her elbows to lift her hips off the desk, kicking off her shoes.

Chase's impatience made him clumsy and Brooke thrilled with the knowledge that he was as affected as she. When at last he managed to yank off her underwear, he wadded it into a ball and tossed it into the far corner of his office, then leaned over her, kissing her deeply and thoroughly before standing and unbuckling his belt.

"Hurry," Brooke whispered in a voice she didn't even recognize.

At that moment the intercom buzzed. It was about five inches from Brooke's head and she yelped.

Chase froze.

The buzz sounded again.

Chase squeezed his eyes shut and took a deep breath, then reached across Brooke to punch a button on the phone console. "Yes?"

"Mr. Davenport, this is Lila downstairs. Your brother and a guest are here to see you."

Brooke stared at Chase. A lock of his hair had fallen over his forehead and his mouth was damp from kissing her.

And then incredibly, she heard him say, "Thank you, Lila. Send them on up."

Brooke bolted upright. "Send them on up? Are you crazy?"

"What was I supposed to say?"

"That you were in a meeting—anything." Brooke pushed against his chest and scrambled off the desk, jerking her skirt down. Dozens of horizontal wrinkles marred the surface. "I can't believe you told them to come up here."

Chase swallowed and ran his fingers through his hair. "I—they'll have to have security badges. It'll take a few minutes."

"Not long enough." Brooke ran around to the side of the desk and found her jacket. Great, but she needed her bra and her blouse first.

Chase had propped his hands on his desktop, his eyes closed.

"Don't just stand there! Look at your desk! Everything's on the floor. And get dressed!" she hissed.

This was a nightmare—like one of those dreams where she was naked in public—only this time it was no dream. She ran toward the other side of the desk at the same time Chase moved. They collided, naked flesh against naked flesh, but there was nothing remotely erotic about the encounter. He gripped her arms to steady her, then brushed past her. Even considering the circumstances, Brooke got a nice little zing out of it.

Brooke's heart was beating so fast she thought it would pound right through her chest—her naked chest. With fumbling fingers, she found her blouse and bra tangled together amidst the pencils, pens and shards of mug. An inch-long smear of ink marred the fabric.

She couldn't worry about that now. Her fingers were sweating with nerves. She ripped the bra from the blouse and shoved her arms through the straps.

Chase was flinging objects back onto his desk.

"Your shirt!" she screeched at him.

"Okay, okay!" He grabbed it and worked at undoing the remaining buttons so he could put it on.

Brooke's bra would *not* fasten. She had to stop and take two calming breaths before successfully hooking it. She put on her blouse and tucked it into her skirt about the time Chase finally got on his shirt and started buttoning it.

Flinging her jacket over one of the club chairs, Brooke started looking for her panties, tossing pens and pencils back on the desk as she did so.

"Where are my panties?"

Chase looked around distractedly. "They've got to be around here somewhere."

"I *know* that!"

There was a discreet knock on the door.

Chase and Brooke froze, then Brooke frantically looked all around for her errant underwear. Just how far could Chase have thrown them, anyway?

CHASE JAMMED his shirttail in his slacks, straightened his desk pad and hoped Jeff wouldn't notice the pens and pencils all over the desk. Then, he headed for the door. At the last minute, he looked at Brooke, who stared back at him, wild-eyed.

Oh, God.

His mind was blessedly numb, but at some point, the numbness was going to wear off and he was going to have to say something. Do something. No, he'd already done quite enough.

Clearly an apology was called for, but there wasn't

time. And he knew a quick, "Sorry," would be insultingly inadequate.

He opened the door. "Hey, Jeff, Courtney." Behind him, he heard a groan.

"How's it goin', man?" Jeff cuffed him on the shoulder.

Chase exhaled. "Oh, you know." He hoped not.

"Hey, Brooke, how's it goin'?" Jeff repeated his greeting.

"Fine!" Brooke answered brightly from the depths of Chase's office.

"Oh, Brooke, we saw soooo many rings!" Courtney laced Jeff's fingers through hers. They kissed.

Chase looked at Brooke, remembering the feel of her mouth against his.

There may have been other high points to his life, but right now he couldn't remember any. He didn't want to remember any. Out of the blue, he'd been given an incredible experience, and just as suddenly, it had been yanked away from him.

He still didn't know how it had happened.

But he sure as hell wanted it to happen again.

What was he thinking! No, he didn't. He didn't maul strange women in his office. He didn't maul strange women anywhere.

He didn't even have a condom with him.

And he hadn't cared. A sick feeling settled in his stomach at the thought. Risking a glance at Brooke, who was casting frantic looks around his office, he wondered what had happened.

She was no more than cute. Appealing, attractive,

sure. But nothing to prompt a man to lose control as he had.

He'd lost his mind, that was it. Just plain lost his mind.

Well, he'd found it now, and just in time to hear Courtney babble on about engagement rings. Apparently, they hadn't bought one.

"But look!" Courtney pulled her hair away from her ear and approached her sister.

Brooke hurriedly crossed the office. "You pierced your ear *again*? Courtney, that's three times!"

"I know, isn't it cool?"

"Be glad it isn't her nose," Chase said.

Everyone looked at him and he wished he hadn't said anything.

"Well, hey," Jeff said. "We came by when we heard Brooke was here. I guess you guys are talking about the wedding, huh?"

"Among other things," Chase murmured.

Brooke didn't meet his eyes.

There was an awkward silence.

"Brooke, I called your office and they said you were here," Courtney said. "So since Jeff and I were downtown anyway, we thought maybe we could all go out to dinner together. You know, get to know each other."

Everybody looked at everybody else.

"There's an Italian place down the block," Chase said reluctantly.

Brooke sent him a withering glance.

What the hell was he supposed to do? He was trying to act normally. Wouldn't going out to eat together be normal?

"Hey, great!" Jeff grinned and he and Courtney kissed again. "We're up for Italian."

"Oh, I don't know . . ." Brooke said.

"Brooooke!" Courtney pleaded. "C'mon!"

"I—I should stop by the office. I left early—"

"So what?" Courtney interrupted. "How many times have you stayed late to interview someone who couldn't get off work? I've eaten dinner all by myself a whole lot lately."

"I know, but I would just feel more comfortable if I stopped by the office." She walked over to Chase's desk. "You all go ahead and I'll call in."

"Call now. We'll wait," Courtney said.

Brooke wore a trapped expression. Clearly, she didn't want to spend anymore time in his company and Chase couldn't blame her.

He had to talk with her about what happened, but what on earth could he say?

"May I use your phone?" she asked him in a voice barely above a whisper.

He felt lower than low. "Sure."

Without looking at him, she reached for it and punched in some numbers, turning so her back was to the room.

Belatedly, Chase remembered the pens and broken mug. He'd rather Jeff and Courtney didn't notice that. "I'll get my jacket."

He deliberately avoided looking at Brooke as he crossed to the coat hook by the ficus tree.

Something white was in the dirt at the base of the tree.

Brooke's panties.

Casually glancing over at Courtney and Jeff, who had their heads together, Chase quickly reached down and slipped the panties into his pocket.

Briefly, he allowed himself to remember the feel of her skin and the taste of her mouth before pulling on his jacket.

Dangerous memories, those. They were memories he shouldn't have because he shouldn't have done what he'd done.

As if that made sense.

He faced Courtney and Jeff in time to hear Courtney say, "You see? I think you think you're more important than you actually are."

"Sometimes people call in after hours."

"Well, tough," Courtney said. "I'm starving."

"It's only five-fifteen," Brooke said. "The restaurant might not even be open. Why don't you all go on, and I'll make a couple of calls here. There are candidates for that clerical position who haven't—"

"Brooke! Lighten up!"

Brooke's face went red, then white, then red again. "Sure. Okay. Let's go." She jammed her arms into her jacket and grabbed her purse.

Chase finally figured out why she was stalling. He had the reason in his pocket.

Duh. He would have figured it out sooner but his brain was still recovering.

He cleared his throat, hoping to catch her attention, but Brooke was determined to ignore him.

He could hardly blame her.

What a mess. What a hideous mess. Still, he owed it to her to let her know he'd found her panties.

He coughed.

No one looked at him.

"Brooke?"

Everyone looked at him.

"Just, ah, making sure dinner is okay with you."

She nodded tightly, still avoiding his eyes.

"Let's go then. I've got everything under control here." Maybe she'd get the message, but from her downcast expression, he guessed not.

"Yeah, everything is a-okay."

They all trooped out of his office.

"Got everything taken care of," he added.

"Well, bully for you," she said through gritted teeth as she marched behind Jeff and Courtney to the elevator.

"And I know you've got everything you came with," he said, but she didn't look back.

The restaurant, Firenze, was about a half block from Chase's office and was wildly expensive, but he didn't care at this point. The three of them were walking ahead of him and he was still trying to figure out a way to let Brooke know he had her panties in his pocket when he suddenly stopped.

He had her panties in his pocket.

She wasn't wearing any underwear.

His reaction was immediate and pronounced.

Don't think of it.

Chase closed his eyes, but when he opened them, he couldn't stop staring at Brooke's bottom, watching as she walked, the gentle sway of her hips just about doing him in.

What was the matter with him?

Until today, he'd been a decent human being. A gentleman. A man who respected women both professionally and personally.

What had happened to him?

Brooke had happened to him, that's what. It was all her fault.

Unable to stop himself, his hand stole into his pocket and he touched the roll of underwear he'd hidden there. As they walked, he unrolled it, remembering how it got rolled in the first place.

What troubled him was that he didn't feel remorseful in the least. Shouldn't he feel regret for what he'd done?

As he watched Brooke walk ahead of him, Chase tried to convince himself that he'd have been better off if this afternoon had never happened.

Try as he might, he couldn't.

5

"COURTNEY, what's going on with them?"

"Shh! Whisper."

"They're acting like they *hate* each other."

"No kidding."

"So, what now?"

"Keep talking about getting married. They're bound to crack sooner or later."

SHE WASN'T wearing underwear. Brooke had never gone out in public without underwear. Ever. She felt exposed. She felt as if everyone knew. She was pretty sure at least one person knew and was mortified because of it.

What must Chase be thinking of her?

When she'd first come into his office, he'd thought she and her sister were opportunists of the worst sort. Now he must think she was a...a... Brooke's mind couldn't even form the word. All she knew was that her underwear was somewhere in the office of a man she'd never met before this afternoon.

How could this have happened?

Firenze was a dressy Italian place. Brooke immediately felt self-conscious about her lack of panty hose—and underwear. Courtney and Jeff were still in teenager casual and they didn't seem concerned, so Brooke tried to appear nonchalant as well.

At least she didn't have to worry about visible panty lines.

As she followed Courtney, Jeff and the hostess across the dining room, Brooke felt parts of her body rubbing together that normally didn't touch. All that touching made her very aware of her walk. A long mirror was on the far wall of the dining room. Brooke stared into it, looking at the man who silently followed them.

Chase walked with his hands shoved into his pockets and his gaze downwards.

On her.

Specifically on her hips.

Unable to help herself, Brooke put a little extra sway into her walk.

No doubt she'd pay for this in some way, but one look at Chase's transfixed expression and she knew the price would be worth it.

They arrived at the table and Courtney and Jeff kissed before sitting down, then kissed once they were seated. They murmured and whispered and held hands while they looked at the menu.

For her part, Brooke concentrated on keeping her knees together and constantly tugged her skirt down. She ignored the man seated on her left. At some point, she and Chase would have to deal with what had happened, but Brooke wanted to do so while wearing underwear.

She'd just chanced releasing the hem of her skirt to open the menu when a voice sang out, "Brooke!"

Startled, she flinched, then waggled her fingers at Doreen Oglesby, her mother's former bridge partner. Doreen left her husband at their table and hurried over to Brooke.

"Oh, just look at you two girls! How are your parents? I've been thinking about them."

"They're fine," Brooke answered, hoping Mrs. Oglesby wasn't going to expect an introduction.

And hoping Courtney and Jeff would keep their hands to themselves. Hoping that Chase wouldn't. Oops. Cancel that.

"I do miss your mama. No one can bid no-trump like she can." Doreen sighed and cast an expectant look around the table.

Might as well get the introductions over with. "Mrs. Oglesby, this is Chase Davenport."

Chase stood and Mrs. Oglesby's eyes lit with a speculative gleam.

Before Brooke could continue, Courtney piped up. "And this is his brother, Jeff Ryan—my fiancé." She gave him a gooey look. Jeff put his arm around her shoulders.

So much for keeping the news quiet.

"Oh, my!" Mrs. Oglesby pressed both hands to her chest.

"Nothing's settled yet," Brooke said quickly, trying for damage control.

"That's why we're here," Courtney said, pretty fast on the uptake, herself.

Brooke glared at her.

"Oh, my!" Mrs. Oglesby repeated. "And I thought I was going to hear interesting news about *you* Brooke. When I saw you walk in, I told Bob something was up. I mean, you're just *glowing.*"

"I'm not glowing," Brooke denied somewhat desperately.

"Well, you're certainly *something.*" Mrs. Oglesby turned to Chase and winked. "Isn't she?"

"She is that."

Glowing. Brooke could *not* look at him. Her emotions were in complete turmoil. For instance, shouldn't she be feeling a little shame? Just a bit? Maybe more than a bit? So why didn't she?

"And *you* are such a handsome man. I don't suppose there is a chance of a double wedding?" At least Mrs. Oglesby was an equal-opportunity embarrasser.

"No!" both Brooke and Chase said together—loudly.

Mrs. Oglesby blinked. Even Jeff and Courtney stopped cooing at each other to look at them.

Both started explanations at the same time.

"Nothing against Chase—"

"Brooke and I just met—"

"We barely know each other."

"Hey, chill, dudes," Jeff said.

Chill, right. Brooke smiled fixedly at Mrs. Oglesby. "It was lovely to see you again."

She took the hint. "Yes, it was. I'll be watching for my invitation to the wedding."

Oh, no. Her parents were bound to hear unless

Brooke stopped this now. "There isn't going to be a wedding—"

"Yes, there is!" Courtney insisted loudly.

"—for a long time," Brooke finished. A long, long, long time.

"Why should we wait?" Jeff asked.

"You both need to finish school—" Chase started to say.

"Who said we weren't going to finish school?"

"Chase meant college," Brooke clarified. "Because Courtney is certainly going to college."

"Here we go again." Courtney crossed her arms over her chest.

"Actually, I meant high school," Chase clarified.

"Gee, thanks for your support," Brooke muttered, finally looking at him.

"One issue at a time," he murmured.

Which, of course, reminded Brooke of another issue, one she had no intention of sharing with her sister.

She looked up to discover Mrs. Oglesby hurrying back to her husband. Great.

"You just *had* to tell her you were engaged," Brooke flung at Courtney.

"Why wouldn't I? I am."

"Did it occur to you that she'll mention it to Mom and Dad?"

"So?"

"So? *So?* You know you shouldn't bother them with this!"

"Bother?" Courtney bristled and clutched Jeff's

hand. "Is that what my wedding is to you? A bother?"

Brooke was aware that she was handling this badly. If only Mrs. Oglesby hadn't been there.

If only she hadn't nearly had a one-afternoon stand with Courtney's future ex-stepbrother-in-law who was sitting *this* close to her.

On the other hand, if they hadn't been interrupted, she wouldn't be so rattled, irritable and on edge right now.

Don't think about that.

She'd also certainly have her underwear.

Don't think about that, either.

Brooke found that as a lifelong underwear wearer, it was more difficult to ignore its absence than she'd thought it would be.

"Jeff, Courtney," Chase said, using an irritatingly reasonable voice. "We only want to make sure you've thought things through."

"What things?" Courtney asked.

"Marriage is a very serious step."

"We *know* that."

"And you're awfully young to want to limit your options."

"What options?" Jeff asked.

"You know…*options.*"

Brooke looked over in time to watch them exchange a look.

"Oh, those options," Jeff said. "Not a problem."

"Do you know what he's talking about?" Courtney asked.

"Kinda." Jeff didn't meet her eyes.

"Well, I don't."

Brooke was afraid she did, but was hoping she didn't. Chase was supposed to be talking about practical matters like apartments, insurance and the cost of living, not reminding Jeff that marriage meant he couldn't date anymore.

"It's like this," Chase leaned forward and looked earnestly at both of them.

Okay. *Now* he'd mention all the dull stuff.

But no.

"You are both entering a time of tremendous change and growth in your lives. You're going to be meeting new people and having new experiences, the sort of experiences that change a person. You'll want to take full advantage of those experiences."

"We can take advantage of them together," Courtney insisted.

"Not necessarily. You'll find that marriage will curtail a lot of your freedom."

Courtney leveled a look at him. "The only freedom that will be *curtailed* will be the freedom to date other people. That's what you're talking about, isn't it?"

"Courtney, give us a break!" Brooke burst out. "You're eighteen and you've known this guy, what? Three weeks? You've spent longer choosing prom dates!"

"We knew each other before the play, but sometimes you just click with a guy. Hasn't that ever happened to you?"

Before this afternoon, Brooke would have responded with an emphatic "no." But now, not only had she recently clicked, the clickee was still within clicking distance. "You can't make that kind of decision based on hormones! They'll get you in trouble every time." She drew a deep breath. "Where is our waitress?"

Courtney sniffed and cuddled next to Jeff. "He doesn't think I'm good enough for you."

"You're *perfect* for me."

"And you're *perfect* for me," Courtney cooed back at him.

This could go on all night and frankly, Chase wasn't being the help Brooke had thought he was going to be. She gave him a warning look, which he met with a look all his own. A look that said, "You're not wearing panties and I know it. And I like it."

At the moment, Brooke kind of liked it, too, but that was wrong, wrong, wrong. They were in the middle of a crisis, or a near crisis, and Chase should be concentrating on not alienating Courtney and Jeff.

Instead, his lips curved upward ever so slightly, just enough to let her know what he was thinking— that if Courtney and Jeff weren't there, then they wouldn't be there either. They'd be back in his office doing wonderfully delicious things....

Rattled, Brooke opened her menu. "Is the lasagna good here? You like lasagna, don't you, Courtney?"

"I usually have the manicotti and it's good," Chase suggested, his voice deceptively mild.

"Then that's what I'll have," Brooke announced brightly, maybe even shrilly.

"I'm just going to have a salad," Courtney said. "I'm cutting back so I'll look good in my wedding dress."

Brooke managed to hold her tongue, but Jeff apparently decided to season the conversation with a little testosterone.

"Good, old predictable Chase, the manicotti man. Every day, the same. No surprises, no fun—"

"Where *is* the waitress?" Brooke swiveled around. Jeff was going to goad Chase into mentioning just how much fun he could work into a day.

"To the immature, being responsible seems boring," Chase commented and took a sip of his water.

"It's stifling!" Courtney burst out. "I'd go nuts if I had to spend every day cooped up in an office."

"I didn't know they gave offices to waitresses," Brooke snapped before she could stop herself.

Courtney smirked. "I'm going to be an actress."

"An actress who makes her living as a waitress." Brooke looked around. "You might apply here. Looks like they need the help."

"There's nothing wrong with being a waitress," Jeff said loyally.

"I'm not saying that there is, only that it's not a career."

"Hel-lo! I'm going to be an actress!"

Brooke changed tacks. "What are you going to be, Jeff?"

He looked startled. "I dunno. But I'm not going to be a suit like Chase."

"How are you planning to support your struggling actress wife?" Chase asked.

"Hey!" Brooke turned to him. "She's going to be pulling her own weight by waitressing! We have yet to hear how Jeff will contribute."

"I'll find something, okay? Jeez." Jeff glowered across the table.

"Looks like you already found something—a hard-working wife!" Brooke observed sarcastically.

"She won't have to work too hard once his trust fund kicks in—if she hangs around that long," Chase snapped.

"Now wait a minute—at least Courtney has dreams and goals. What does Jeff have?"

"Me—to guide him."

"Oh, *that's* reassuring."

"Man, I told you, it's my life—"

"Just stop it—stop it all of you!" Courtney began to cry. "This was s-supposed to be a celebration and you've ruined it!" Pushing back her chair, she got up from the table and ran in the direction of the rest rooms.

Jeff started to get up, too, but Brooke shook her head. "I'll go talk to her." She reached for her napkin to put it beside her place and felt Chase's hand on her thigh.

Startled, she gasped. The nerve of him. Except that he had a strangely intent look on his face as he bumped her hand with his. Brooke glanced down as Chase's fingers opened to reveal a ball of white.

Her panties.

Mortified, Brooke grabbed them as her face burned with heat so intense she expected to pop a blood vessel.

She couldn't just walk through the restaurant carrying them in her hand, so she reached for her purse and jammed them inside. Mumbling something she hoped Chase would interpret as a sentiment appropriate for an inappropriate event she then fled the table.

There were only two stalls in the rest room and soft sobs were coming from one of them.

"Courtney?"

"How *could* you, Brooke?"

"I'm sorry. We got started wrong and—"

"Most sisters would be glad to be included in wedding plans."

"I am, I am." At all costs, Brooke needed to keep the lines of communication open.

She couldn't believe how badly she and Chase had handled this. They'd planned their strategy and instead of following it, had ended up insulting each other's family. And giving each other hot looks.

Snuffling, Courtney pushed open the stall door and went to the sink. Turning on the tap, she rinsed her face with cold water. "Do you have any mascara with you?"

Sure. In her purse right underneath her panties. "You know it's not a good idea to share makeup."

Courtney looked at her as though Brooke had grown horns. "I am your sister!"

Brooke barely opened her purse and dug around

until she found the tube. Then she went into the stall. There wasn't much room for maneuvering inside and she didn't particularly want to take off her shoes. Ick.

Brooke hitched up her skirt and sat down, then had a thought. Courtney might not see the reflection of her feet in the mirror if she were distracted.

"You remember when Chase said that he was guiding Jeff?"

"Guiding? Ha. Chase has taken over his life. He has college all lined up, Jeff's major chosen and a summer job waiting for him. He's trying to make Jeff into a clone of himself. Jeff doesn't want that."

Talking about Jeff was as good a distraction as she was going to get, Brooke thought. Leaning back, she quietly raised her foot and carefully worked it through a leg hole, trying not to catch the heel of her pump.

Her panties were a stretchy, unadorned, white cotton. They couldn't be plainer.

They couldn't be more unsexy.

If she had to leave underwear in a man's office, why couldn't it be a lacy thong?

On the other hand, why was she more upset by her white underwear than the fact that it had been left anywhere?

"I mean, Chase is an okay guy, I guess," Courtney continued, oblivious, "but all he does is work. Jeff says he doesn't get home until eight o'clock every night, and that's only if he doesn't stop by the gym first. He almost always goes into his office on the weekends and works on stuff at home, too. He never has any fun."

Oh, yes he does. "So I guess that means he doesn't have a girlfriend."

"When would he have time? He's like you. Work, work, work all the time."

"I don't work *all* the time and Chase probably doesn't either."

Now for the tricky part. Brooke leaned back struggling to bend her knee and keep everything above the bottom of the door so Courtney wouldn't see.

"Can I borrow your brush, too?" Courtney's hand appeared under the door of the stall.

It startled Brooke and she missed the leg opening and caught her heel on the edge of her panties. She pulled her leg back and the momentum propelled her elbow into the stall's metal side. "Ow!"

"What are you doing in there?"

Wincing, Brooke rubbed her funny bone. "Trying to get my purse." She did so and handed her brush to Courtney, then leaned back once again.

Too far. Her back hit the metal flushing button on the wall and with an enthusiastic roar, it flushed.

"No!" Brooke jumped up, but was too late. Water had splashed over her jacket and skirt.

"Brooke...are you okay?"

"No, I'm not okay!" Brooke tugged her panties up and her skirt down and emerged from the stall. It was worse than she'd thought.

"What happened?"

"I got wet."

"Well, yeah, but—"

"Just get some paper towels."

"There aren't any." Courtney gestured to the hand dryers on the wall.

"Oh, great."

"But the dryers are better. Give me your jacket."

Brooke had no choice and while Courtney kept one dryer going, Brooke held her skirt over the other.

"You've got ink on your blouse!" Courtney shouted over the roar that echoed through the tiled rest room. "I guess it's just not your day for clothes."

Brooke knew it was only a matter of time before someone else entered the rest room. Even though it was early, the restaurant was crowded with people who were eating dinner before going to the theater.

At least she had underwear to stand around in now.

Sure enough, a woman wandered in and gave Brooke a sympathetic glance. "Wine?"

Brooke shook her head. "Water."

"Well, that's lucky."

Yeah, real lucky.

After the woman left, Courtney, who'd been uncharacteristically silent, ventured a comment. "You've been acting weird ever since we met you in Chase's office. What's up?"

"Weird just because I don't want to see my sister tie herself down right out of high school?"

Courtney's face turned mutinous and Brooke wished she'd kept quiet.

"I don't want to go to college—I don't need all those extra courses. I want to study acting at film school, and since you'll convince Mom and Dad that's a bad idea, why shouldn't I get married? What else am I going to do?"

And Brooke spoke the words she never thought she would, the words she'd warned Courtney about only this morning. "Why don't you just live together?"

"Brooke!" Courtney's dryer stopped. "I'm going to tell Mom and Dad you said that!" Her voice echoed.

"Please don't." Brooke was already sorry she'd suggested it. She reached over and punched the button on Courtney's dryer.

"Anyway, Jeff gets some of his trust fund when he gets married."

Though her hands were burning from the heat of the dryer, Brooke's blood ran cold. "You knew about the trust fund?"

"Of course."

Her sister *was* a gold digger. "You're marrying him for his money?"

"Don't be silly. He's marrying *me* for his money."

"That distinction doesn't make it a whole lot better."

"Well, what do you and Chase expect us to do?"

Brooke was nearly speechless. "I can't believe you're marrying the first available man—no, boy, because Jeff is still a boy—and throwing your future away."

"It's *my* future!"

"But you've got such opportunities! Opportunities I never had."

"I don't want your opportunities!"

"Courtney, be reasonable."

The dryer clicked off. Courtney examined the jacket. "It's still damp, but it's not so noticeable. Here." She thrust it at Brooke, then ran from the rest room.

Brooke wiggled into her skirt—had the dryer shrunk it?—grabbed her jacket and purse and followed Courtney back into the restaurant.

One look at their table told her that Chase and Jeff had held a similar conversation during their absence. Chase sat, arms folded across his chest, jaw muscle working as he gritted his teeth, and stared at Jeff, who was comforting Courtney.

Brooke had had enough. "Please. If you're trying to convince me that you're a good actress, this isn't cutting it."

"Oh, nice one," Chase said.

"Can't you see what she's doing?"

"Yes, but I wouldn't have mentioned it."

"No, your style is to tell your brother he can do better."

"I didn't say that."

"Not in so many words, but now that you bring it up—"

"They're fighting again!" Courtney wailed into Jeff's shoulder. "Take me home!"

"Yeah, let's get out of here."

Their waitress finally appeared. "Are y'all ready to order?"

"No," Chase said. "We've lost our appetites."

6

"THEY HATE EACH OTHER."

"I know, isn't it great?"

"But I thought you wanted them to get together."

"Jeff, you've got to be more flexible. The more uncomfortable and worried they are, the more likely we are to get our own way, which had better be soon because Valentine's Day is coming up and I've got to get that application in the mail."

"I'm just not good at this stuff."

"You are, too! You're playing the boyfriend part *very* well."

"Yeah?"

"Yeah."

BROOKE ARRIVED home first and wasted no time in stripping off her clothes and getting into the shower. She didn't take an especially long time, but Courtney should have been home by the time she got out. She wasn't.

Brooke couldn't believe that disaster of a dinner. She and Chase had made plans—what had happened to those? They'd said all the wrong things. They'd been confrontational when they should have been pragmatic. They'd lost their heads and had given in to their emotions.

Again.

Brooke dressed in her comfort sweats and started making salads for dinner, trying to convince herself that Courtney wouldn't do anything stupid.

Like her sister.

No. Brooke hacked at a poor defenseless carrot. Not stupid. Unexpected. And she was glad it had happened. Glad.

She'd been too complacent recently and this... encounter with Chase was just what she needed to not only make her sympathize with Courtney, but to remind her what could happen when emotions got the better of her.

And that's exactly what she intended to tell Chase when she spoke with him.

She'd finished castrating the carrot, stabbing a tomato and ripping a head of lettuce before Courtney came through the kitchen door. Brooke was behind the open refrigerator door and saw Courtney glance toward the chopping block before she noticed Brooke. At least she hadn't been crying.

"Hi," Brooke said quietly.

"Hey." Courtney wandered over to the kitchen table. "Is that dinner?"

"Yeah, just something light."

"Thanks." Courtney sat at her normal place and waited for Brooke to finish setting the table.

Brooke tried not to feel irritated and heaven knew this wasn't the time to prod Courtney into lending a hand, but how could she expect Brooke to treat her as a fellow adult when she still acted like an entitled child?

Yes, Courtney had to fend for herself at dinner on those days when Brooke worked late, but why hadn't it occurred to her to fix them *both* dinner? Brooke would have loved to come home to a meal she didn't have to fix herself.

A suspicious sniff interrupted her thoughts. Pouring two glasses of iced tea, Brooke brought them to the table.

Head down, Courtney mumbled, "Thanks," and sniffed again.

"Are you crying?" Brooke would have bet her entire 401-K plan that Courtney had been fine when she'd arrived home.

Courtney raised her head, wiping at the corner of her eye too fast for Brooke to see if there had been an actual tear there or not. It was a good effect anyway. Maybe Courtney did have a future as an actress.

"After what happened at dinner, wouldn't you cry?"

"I was there, and I'm not crying."

"Think about it Brooke! You and Chase *hate* each other! You are the people closest to Jeff and me. How are we supposed to plan a wedding when our families can't stand each other?"

"We don't hate each other."

"Oh, come on. You could barely look at him. And the things you said—"

"Were said in the heat of the moment. I'll admit

that we...weren't..." Brooke waved her hand, seeking the right words, "as calm and rational as I would have liked, but you've got to admit that you and Jeff pushed some hot buttons."

"But we want you two to get along."

Privately, Brooke didn't think it was necessary that she and Chase get along, but she smiled and nodded for Courtney's sake.

"And we think all you need to do is to get to know each other better."

Better than what? Brooke thought. On the other hand, they did need to meet again so they could attempt to give Jeff and Courtney a dose of reality. But on her turf this time. "Okay, Courtney. Why don't you invite Jeff and his brother over here and we'll talk about this."

"You mean our wedding."

Be cool. "Yes, among other things," she couldn't help adding.

"Okay—hey, I know! We'll invite them for dinner." Courtney looked delighted with herself. But she would, having no idea of the work required.

"I don't know . . ." Brooke didn't want the stress of cooking for them all.

"I'll cook."

"*You'll* cook?"

"Sure."

"Courtney, you don't know how to cook."

"Of course I do. How do you think I eat when you're not here?"

Brooke was about to point out the difference between microwaving a frozen meal for one and a dinner party for four, but thought better of it. "They do have those frozen family-size main dish meals. The lasagna isn't bad."

"Oh, ick. I couldn't serve them frozen lasagna after Chase tried to take us to Firenze!"

"Good point. So pick up a roast chicken—"

"No." Courtney straightened, looking determined. "I'm going to cook a real meal. Myself. I don't want to give Chase anything else to criticize me for."

Talk about snatching victory from the jaws of defeat. What a break for Brooke. Courtney had no idea what she was getting into.

It was a perfect opportunity to demonstrate to her that she wasn't ready for domestic responsibility.

"Great idea," Brooke told her. "They do say that the way to a man's heart is through his stomach." What was with her and clichés today?

"I'm not aiming for his heart," Courtney said. "He doesn't have one."

Unbidden, memories of Chase's heart beating against her lips floated through Brooke's mind. She remembered the touch of his hands and feel and smell of his skin.

They were absolutely going to have to talk before he and Jeff came to dinner.

CHASE SAT in front of the computer in his home office, but instead of working, he'd been surfing the Internet looking for information on hormonal disorders.

The rumble of the automatic garage door announced Jeff's arrival. Finally. Chase clicked over to the CNN home page and waited for his stepbrother to come charging into the room.

"Chase!"

"In here," Chase called, not relishing the coming confrontation.

Jeff burst into the room, removed his school letter jacket, and tossed it toward a chair. "I don't know what was up with dinner, but you are not going to disrespect Courtney!"

So it was serious. Chase had expected whining, complaining and wheedling. He hadn't expected to confront a man defending the honor of his woman. It was the first time he'd sensed maturity in Jeff. Too bad this was the occasion.

And too bad Jeff was absolutely correct. "I'm sorry. It was not my intention to insult your girlfriend."

"Fiancée," Jeff said belligerently.

This wasn't the time to argue semantics. "Fiancée," Chase corrected.

"*Or* her sister. You weren't too nice to Brooke, either."

"Brooke and I..." What could he say?

"Hate each other," Jeff supplied.

"No, not hate." Definitely not hate.

"Well, you don't like each other and that's too bad, because you're going to be in-laws. So you'd better come up with a way you can get along with her."

As Jeff finished speaking, the telephone rang. Without asking, he reached across Chase's desk and snatched up the receiver.

The anger instantly melted from his face and Chase knew Courtney was calling.

"Sure, that'd be great! Yeah. Okay. Love you, too. Love you more. No, love *you* more. No, love *you*—"

He broke off when Chase threatened to disconnect the call. "Gotta go!" He made a kissing noise into the phone and hung up. "Hey, guess what?"

"I have no idea."

"See? You gotta ditch this attitude." The familiar teenage Jeff was back. "Courtney and Brooke invited us to dinner. Courtney's going to cook. I said we'd go. Is that okay?"

"When?"

"I don't know. Sometime."

"Well, find out!"

"Chill." Jeff reached for his jacket. "It's not like you've got any other plans."

"I could have plans."

"Yeah, sure."

"I don't tell you all the details of my day, Jeff. But as it happens, I'm waiting on a bid for a property in Atlanta. And I might have to take off for Colorado next week," he added for good measure.

"Anything other than work?"

Chase was silent.

Jeff shrugged into his jacket. "Dinner'll probably be Saturday, since we've got play rehearsal after school the rest of the week." Jeff paused at the doorway. "And this time, try to be nice."

It was a good thing Chase had decided to cut Jeff a lot of slack.

He wished he could do the same for himself. Flipping back over to his hormone research, he read the articles he'd bookmarked, then tried searching for "sexual attraction" but only ended up with about a million porn sites. Even if there was some scholarly research paper on the subject, it would be buried in the list. Not ready to give up, Chase narrowed the search by typing in "doctor" and "paper" and ended up with eye-opening sites featuring doctor-paper gown fantasies, doctors doing nonmedical things with various medical instruments and an exterminator site offering flypaper for sale.

Now he was ready to give up, but he was still going to have to talk to Brooke before they all met for dinner.

And just what was he going to say?

He felt a little guilty about what had happened in his office, he supposed, but honestly, not guilty enough. In fact, if he were really honest, he'd admit that he didn't feel guilty at all. His only concern was Brooke and what *she* felt. It was important that she know he'd never done anything like that before.

He guessed he needed to apologize, but he didn't want to do that either. The thing was, he wasn't sorry. The timing was off, the circumstances were off, but the chemistry was right on. And frankly, great chemistry didn't come his way often enough to ignore.

The reaction between them had been instantaneous and their argument at dinner had been an attempt to neutralize it. Brooke had felt the same way, he knew it.

He still couldn't believe her explosive response— or his, for that matter. It was like some kind of cheesy fantasy.

He couldn't get it out of his mind, and that was the problem. An apology would imply regret. And the only thing he regretted was that he wasn't at a point in his life when he could offer Brooke anything more. How was he supposed to say that?

By the next morning, Chase knew that whatever he was going to say had to be said in person. Deliberately arriving at his office before the clerical staff, he looked in the direction of his desk.

The night cleaning crew had cleared away the broken mug and had put the rest of his papers and stray pens back on his desk, but hadn't arranged anything.

Chase closed his eyes and allowed himself to relive a few minutes of the most erotic experience of his life before putting everything back the way it had been before Brooke had walked in.

He needed a new mug for his pencils and pens, but he had plenty over by the coffeepot. Snagging a green one, he filled it, smoothed out the new creases on his desk pad and wasted the next hour trying to figure out what to say.

He was going to have to say it in person—he'd decided that already. Maybe he'd think of the right words on the way to Brooke's office.

Chase found himself in the lobby of Brooke's building, still without the slightest idea of what he was going to say. And realized that Brooke's reaction would determine a lot of it.

BROOKE DIDN'T HAVE any interviews scheduled for this morning and couldn't decide if that was a good or a bad thing.

On the good side, she wouldn't be distracted from properly screening job candidates. On the bad side, she was getting absolutely nothing accomplished.

She and Chase had to talk before Saturday night. Twice, she'd picked up the telephone, but each time she'd put it back down. She wasn't ready. Would she *ever* be ready?

With a deep breath she reached for the phone a third time.

Her fingers just touched it when it rang, startling her. Saved by the bell, it seemed.

Or not.

"Brooke?"

It was Chase. Her stomach went into an immediate free fall. "H-hello."

"Are you free to talk for a couple of minutes?"

"Yes. In fact, I was just going to call you."

"Well...I'd like to meet with you."

Brooke squeezed her eyes shut. "Is that such a good idea?"

"What I have to say needs to be said in person."

Her stomach landed with a thud. "Sure." She drew her appointment calendar toward her. "What time?"

There was a hesitation. "Now? I'm in the lobby."

A vast unblemished white area stretched all the way until one-thirty. "Okay. I'm in suite fourteen thirty-two."

"See you in a few minutes."

A few minutes. *A few minutes.* Brooke's pulse jumped. She needed more than a few minutes to prepare herself to see Chase again. How was she supposed to act? How did he want her to act? No. She should be asking herself how *she* wanted to act. No that wasn't it—she should be asking herself how she was *supposed* to act. That was better.

So, how was she supposed to act?

Because she couldn't stand sitting in her office and waiting for him, Brooke went out to the reception area.

Her eyes met Chase's as soon as the elevator doors opened.

She'd forgotten that he was actually a good-looking man. It was a sneaky handsomeness—obviously—the kind that wasn't noticeably striking. The kind that snuck up on a girl.

Add that to the fact that he was wearing a suit and she had a weakness for men in suits and...well, she shouldn't be so hard on herself for yesterday.

"My office is this way," she said, proud of the way her voice was coolly polite for the benefit of both Chase and the typing pool outside her door.

Her office was little more than a glorified cubicle. There was barely enough room for her file cabinet, her desk, an extra chair and a silk palm with leaves that had faded on the window side. Still, Brooke was proud that she had a door she could close. Which she did.

"Have a seat." She returned to her side of the desk, glad that there wasn't a choice about it.

She got settled and found that Chase was watching her. What? Did he expect her to pounce on him? Probably.

They looked at each other. She tried to read Chase's expression and keep hers impassive at the same time, then realized he was undoubtedly doing the same thing.

Finally, he smiled slightly. "I came here so we could talk about yesterday."

She nodded. "That's what I thought." She had a mental image of them in a sparring ring, circling around, waiting for the other to deliver the first punch.

"Are you all right?"

The question hung in the air. Chase watched her intently. Brooke supposed there could be all sorts of legal ramifications, if that was what she wanted. She didn't, but he couldn't know that. "Yeah, sure," she lied.

"I'm not."

That wasn't what she'd expected. She'd thought he'd look relieved. "You're not?"

He made a gesture with his hands. "I don't know what to say about it."

Brooke knew exactly what "it" was. "What do you want to say?"

"Something that doesn't insult you, or make me look like an opportunistic jerk. How about you?"

She laughed. "I'd like to come up with something that doesn't make me sound too prudish or too easy."

"Hey—no. I realize you're not like that."

A beat went by. "Define 'that.'"

A wary look crossed his face. "Ah...you know."

"Sexy? Uninhibited? Wild? Daring? A good-time girl?" She couldn't force herself to say the *s* word.

"You see?" He gestured with his index finger. "This is what I knew would happen. Anything I say will be the wrong thing. Do you want me to apologize? Because I will, if that's what you want."

No, she didn't want. But shouldn't he want? "Why *haven't* you apologized?"

Chase got to his feet, propped his hands on her desk and leaned forward, holding her gaze with his. "Because I'm not sorry." He straightened. "So sue me." Then he swallowed. "That was rhetorical."

"Understood." Like she wanted to explain *her* behavior in court.

He paced the three steps that her office allowed. "Brooke, I've never done anything like that before. I've never wanted to." He continued pacing. "There was just such a visceral attraction—you felt it." He stopped in front of her desk. "Tell me you felt it."

Brooke was loving the word "visceral." She nodded and he paced again.

"I knew it. I knew it couldn't be one-sided." He pivoted and stopped in front of her desk again. "It was the sexiest thing that's ever happened to me. *You* are the sexiest thing that's ever happened to me."

And Brooke felt a visceral reaction, that's for sure. She probably shouldn't like being described as a "sexiest thing" quite so much.

"It was lust. Pure lust. Pure raw jam-it-anywhere

lust." He stopped pacing and looked at her. "Did I say that out loud?"

"Yes."

Chase studied her. "You don't look as offended as you should."

"Truth?"

He nodded.

"I'm not. Incredibly, I'm not. In fact, I think that pretty much sums up how I felt, too. I couldn't even think—I didn't care what I was doing. It was just this overwhelming..."

"Lust."

"Lust," she repeated.

He was back in front of her desk. "I can't stop thinking about it. About you."

"But especially it."

He nodded, looking serious. "Unlike my marriage-minded brother, I'm not ready for a relationship. Also, unlike Jeff, I believe that a strong relationship takes time and work. And I'm absolutely willing to give it that."

"I hear a 'but.'"

"But right now, I don't have the time and I don't have the energy. You see, my dad wasn't around much when I was growing up and I've promised myself that it won't be like that for my kids. I'm going to earn a nice, fat, financial cushion now so I can ease up later. I figure it'll take another two years."

It was a kiss-off without the kiss. She was "the sexiest thing" that had ever happened to him, but it wasn't enough to knock him off his future path. She wasn't even worth a detour.

Not that she wanted to be a detour. She should be grateful for his honesty.

Still she wanted to dish out a little herself. "I know what you mean." Brooke tried not to notice the relief on his face. "I don't have time for a relationship, either. And casual encounters aren't my style." He needed to know that just in case he was going to suggest something icky that she would have to turn down. But then, she'd be tempted to call him in the middle of the night and show up at his place wearing high heels and a trench coat.

He spoiled it all. "There was nothing casual about our encounter."

"But that's all it's going to be, right? *An* encounter?"

"Is that what you want?" His eyes searched her face.

"I think that would be best," Brooke answered.

"I don't." His voice was all husky and low and filled with promise.

Brooke put her hands over her ears. "Stop saying things like that! It's over. Done. Never to be repeated."

"Can you just forget about it that easily?"

She noticed they kept saying "it" instead of "you," "me" and "sex." "Who said anything about forgetting?"

"Exactly."

Brooke was just about to point out that she ought to

be worth squeezing out a little time and energy for and that knowing he didn't think she merited a spot in his very busy schedule had cooled a lot of the lust she'd previously felt.

"You know, I think part of the reason we can't forget it is because we were interrupted before it came to its natural conclusion."

"Can you stop calling it 'it'?" Here came the let's-finish-what-we-started suggestion. Brooke was simultaneously thrilled and disappointed.

"So what should I call it? The groping session?" He used his fingers to make quote marks. "The 'kiss'? The quickie? Afternoon delight? It was a little late to call it a nooner."

"How about sexual harassment?" she snapped.

That stopped him. "I thought it was mutual."

"It was." Why did she have to be so darn truthful? "By the way, I've changed my mind. 'It' will be fine."

"What were we talking about?" he asked.

"Natural conclusions being interrupted."

"Yeah." He rubbed the back of his neck. "Because we were interrupted, we only have these hot memories of each other."

"Incredibly hot."

"And there was an element of newness, too."

"The thrill of discovery."

He shot her a guarded look. "My theory is that nothing can live up to our memory of the way it was, but we don't *know* that for sure."

"So our imaginations are running away with us,

conjuring up all sorts of intense feelings, invading our daydreams, haunting our nights?"

"Something like that." His eyes looked glazed.

He was such an easy target, Brooke should be ashamed of herself. "And you propose what?"

"That we do it again."

"No. No," she repeated, when her insides went into their melting act. She stood and prepared to open the door in a last desperate act of self-preservation. "I think that is a very bad idea."

"Please hear me out." Chase stepped in front of her, blocking her way. "Please."

A man was pleading with her. Begging, even. And darn it, Brooke hadn't experienced enough begging men in her life, especially not those who had previously attributed their raw, animal lust to her. She said nothing. If he said 'please' again in that scratchy half whisper, then maybe—

"Please?" he said in a scratchy half whisper.

Ooh, more melting. "Okay. Say what you've got to say."

"It's simple. We're obsessing about—"

"Correction. *I'm* not obsessing—just thinking about it a lot."

Irritation crossed his face. "*I'm* obsessing, then. Me. All by myself. Obsessing."

"You're cute when you're obsessed."

Chase was surprised into a laugh.

"That's better," Brooke said. "You were getting a little intense."

He reached out and cupped the side of her face. "You see what you do to me?"

And she felt the jolt all the way to her toes.

"I can't go on like this."

Brooke was very much afraid that she could.

"So let's get this out of our system." He held up a finger when she started to protest. "For just a minute. For a single minute, we'll give in to this..." He gestured as he struggled for the right word.

"'It'?" Brooke asked.

"Yes, 'it.' For one minute. I'll set the alarm on my watch."

She hesitated, then heard herself say, "Three."

When he raised an eyebrow, she elaborated. "I have a lot of inner tension to discharge."

"Me, too." He smiled. "Five."

"Go for it." Brooke could already feel some of that inner tension winding up at just the thought of kissing Chase again.

Chase pulled and pushed at the knobs on his watch. Brooke heard a tiny beep.

"Is it set?"

He raised his eyes. "Yes."

For an instant, neither of them moved.

Then they were in each other's arms.

And it was even better than before. But it wasn't supposed to be better—he'd promised. Well, he hadn't exactly promised...it had been more of a theory...

It was the familiarity of his mouth. The first-time newness was gone and in its place was the richness of experience. She remembered the movements of her tongue that had made him sigh his pleasure. She remembered the feel of his shoulders beneath her hands, the feel of his arms holding her close.

And she remembered the urgent haste to get as close as possible to each other.

Five minutes they'd decided?

AND HE'D originally thought one minute would be enough to eradicate the memories of the feel of her from his every waking moment. She hadn't believed him. Smart girl.

He couldn't believe Brooke was back in his arms and it was every bit as great as he remembered. Better, even.

Her mouth, her response, her body, her skin, her scent, her taste...he was drowning in her. If he didn't come up for air soon, he'd be a goner.

His hands wandered over her back and flirted with the waistband of her skirt under her jacket. He should have asked that she take it off first. Except—they were only supposed to be kissing, weren't they? He'd promised only kissing, hadn't he?

Hadn't he?

One way to find out. He jerked her blouse out of her skirt waistband and ran his fingers over her back, then unhooked her bra.

Her only response was a shudder and he'd never been so happy in his entire life. "Brooke," he murmured, filling his hand with her breast.

She gasped into his mouth.

He couldn't get enough of her. He'd never be able to get enough of her, but right now, she was in his arms and he wasn't going to think about it anymore.

Chase surrendered to the sensations that made every nerve in his body burn with pleasure. He tried to share it with Brooke, learning that her excited response fueled his own.

He wanted her—and for far longer than the five minutes he'd arrogantly allotted. Plunging his fingers through the thick hair he'd imagined spread over his pillow, Chase angled her head so that he could kiss her more deeply. As he lost himself in the pleasure of her mouth, alarm bells sounded.

Danger, danger, danger.

Alarm bells...alarm...a beeping penetrated his consciousness.

The alarm on his watch was going off.

Maybe Brooke didn't hear it.

But since his wrist was right by her ear, she did. He felt her withdraw and had no choice but to do likewise. That had been the agreement.

Slowly, Chase pulled away, unable to resist pressing a last kiss on her forehead. She could interpret that however she wanted.

"Are you sure you set that thing for five minutes?" Her breathing was gratifyingly ragged.

"More or less." Mostly more. He'd rounded up.

They stepped away from each other.

"Would you...?" She twirled her finger around.

"Oh—sure." Chase turned his back and had to endure the sounds of her straightening her clothes.

"Okay." She pulled a couple of tissues from the dispenser on her desk and handed one to him. "Lipstick."

He wiped at his mouth and watched her do the same.

She looked entirely too calm.

He couldn't stand it. "Well?"

"Yeah. Great plan." She wadded the tissue into a ball and tossed it into the wastebasket. Two points. "It worked. That kiss was nothing like before."

His plan had worked? It wasn't supposed to work that well. Secretly he hadn't wanted it to work at all. And it hadn't worked for him, not by a long shot. He'd been ready to smash his geeky techno watch—a Christmas present from Jeff—against the wall as soon as the first beep sounded. Or as soon as he'd been conscious of the beeping. The thing probably hadn't given the full five minutes, either.

The kiss had been nothing like before? What did she mean? If anything, he'd been better than before, motivated by the knowledge that it was supposed to be the last time. And she'd moaned. He'd distinctly heard a moan. From nothing to moaning well within five minutes was pretty damn good, if he did say so himself.

How could she just *sit* there?

"We should talk about Courtney and Jeff," she said.

"Sure." Why? Why should they talk about Courtney and Jeff? He wanted to talk about them. Only there was no them.

Not only had he told her so, he knew so.

This was nothing more than physical attraction no matter how intense. It was a flash fire that would burn itself out just as quickly as it started.

Just as it had been with his father and Jeff's mother.

The thought had come from nowhere, but Chase knew it was true. All these years he'd despised his father for his weakness over Zoe, who had been absolutely nothing like Chase's mother.

"Chase?"

He looked at Brooke and felt the fire within him build again.

But he wasn't his father and he wouldn't give into it. Standing, he said, "I think if we just stick to our original plan of matter-of-factly pointing out all the practical details of married life, it will give them something to think about."

Brooke nodded, sending her hair rippling against her shoulder. "We should make an effort to keep calm and unemotional about it." She looked straight at him. "Emotions just get in the way. They cause all kinds of trouble and people end up doing things they shouldn't."

Chase got the message. "Agreed."

Their eyes held a moment longer. Everything in him was screaming for him to ask—no beg—for another five minutes. Another five hours. Another five days, another five anything.

But instead, he forced himself to turn the doorknob and leave her office. He walked all the way to the elevator, punched the button and got in, all without looking back. Once the doors closed, he slumped against the back wall.

He was in such trouble.

BROOKE HELD HERSELF together until she was certain Chase was truly gone. Then she went limp, slumping back in her chair, closing her eyes and reliving those last five minutes in his arms.

She'd never felt that way before and she had an awful feeling she never would again.

7

"Courtney, are you sure you know what you're doing?"

"Sort of."

"This is the weirdest food I've ever seen. In fact, I'm not sure it *is* food. Do you know how many stores I had to go to before I could find quince?"

"It'll be worth it."

"What is all this stuff?"

"Aphrodisiacs."

"No kidding."

"Nope. Want a taste?"

"Uh, no, 'cause, I, uh need to go get that stuff from my mom's storage unit now."

"Chicken."

"I'd taste chicken."

Courtney needed the full domestic cooking experience, Brooke felt, so she arranged to be away from the house a good part of Saturday morning. And afternoon.

She got her hair trimmed, and on impulse treated herself to a manicure. After that, she went to the mall and window-shopped. And then she really shopped. The merchants were really pushing Valentine's Day.

Normally, Brooke avoided stores around that day, since not having a Valentine made her cranky. And she still didn't have a Valentine.

She had Chase. Or no, she didn't have Chase. They'd made the very mature decision not to have each other.

And, truthfully, Brooke was the tiniest bit miffed that he'd been able to make the decision so easily.

He should have suffered over the decision. She wanted him to suffer. She wanted validation, she wanted him panting at her feet, she wanted...

She wanted all her escaped hormones to go back into deep freeze, that's what she wanted. It hadn't been easy to freeze them the first time and they were doing a darned good job of eluding capture this time around.

In the midst of all her internal angst, a dress called to her. She distinctly heard her name. "Brooke!" Or it could have been saying "broke," which was what she was after buying the red slip dress. It wasn't even on sale. When was the last time she'd bought something for herself that wasn't on sale?

Or red? She had no red in her closet and she certainly had no shoes to go with this dress.

This time there was a sale, but since she bought two pairs of shoes, including a pair of completely impractical red high-heeled sandals, she spent just as much money.

It must have been the Valentine's Day influence. Decorations were everywhere, along with expensive chocolate...and lingerie.

Brooke stopped in front of the potpourri-scented store and stared at the display in the window.

Thongs. Red thongs. Red silk thongs.

All she could think about was her comfortable, but plain, white panties—the kind a mother always wanted her daughter to wear in the event of an unexpected trip to the emergency room. Those were the panties Chase had rescued from his office.

Maybe sexiness wasn't supposed to be comfortable, Brooke decided after leaving the store with a thong she'd tried on, but bought anyway.

And then she turned around, went back inside and bought the matching cleavage-enhancing bra.

After that, she headed home, afraid she'd buy something else totally and completely un-Brooke-like. The sparkly red heart earrings at the jewelry minicart by the food court for instance.

Food. She'd missed lunch and with Courtney cooking, it wouldn't be wise to show up hungry for dinner. Brooke detoured to the food court and bought a pita sandwich.

And the sparkly red heart earrings.

Then she went home.

It didn't take long for the guilt to kick in. She shouldn't have left Courtney to fix dinner all by herself. She shouldn't have spent all that money on herself. Where was she going to wear that dress? Those shoes? That underwear?

Well...there was always tonight.

No, not tonight! Why should she wear a slinky dress and a thong just because she was going to see

Chase? There was no way he'd even know about the thong.

Besides, tonight's meeting wasn't about seeing Chase again, it was about Courtney and Jeff and their rampaging hormones.

And speaking of hormones, when Brooke arrived home, she saw the Honda sitting out front, which meant Jeff was there.

Brooke walked into the kitchen prepared for a disaster, which was a good thing, because that's exactly what she found.

Dirty dishes, strange boxes and jars with foreign labels were spread all over the kitchen. In the middle of it all, not looking the slightest bit fazed, were Courtney and Jeff.

"Hi, Brooke!" Courtney beamed a smile at her. "Oooh, you've been shopping. What did you buy?"

"A dress and shoes," Brooke mumbled.

Courtney and Jeff exchanged a look. Why? What was that for?

"Going to wear them tonight?" Courtney asked.

They thought she'd bought the clothes for Chase's benefit. Well, she hadn't. No. Not at all.

But why shouldn't she wear the red dress? And the shoes. And the... "I was planning to. Why? Are you serving messy food?"

Courtney laughed. "Maybe. We're serving strange, exotic and wonderful food."

Before Brooke could establish exactly what Courtney considered strange, exotic and wonderful, Jeff called out, "Hey, Courtney." He carried a saucepan over to her. "Do you think it's supposed to look this way?"

"The recipe *said* stir until the liquid coats a spoon."

"Yeah, but were they talking about a ski jacket or a raincoat?"

Brooke chose that moment to quietly leave the kitchen. She passed by the dining room and saw that the table wasn't set yet. After she put away her new clothes, she'd volunteer for that chore. But that was before she saw the den.

The furniture had been rearranged with the chairs and sofa pushed to the walls and the coffee table pulled to the middle of the room. Surrounding it were large floor pillows that Brooke had never seen before. They were in an opulent ethnic print of cinnamon, saffron, paprika and chocolate. A gold-threaded fabric runner covered the coffee table and coordinating place mats and napkins set off plates and bowls that were also new. The only thing Brooke recognized was the silverware.

A fortune in votive candles marched down the center of the table, across the fireplace mantel, on the lamp tables and on any other available surface. And the centerpiece—Brooke walked all the way around the table admiring the sumptuous display of leaves and fruit.

And she'd thought Courtney wouldn't be able to handle a dinner for four.

"What do you think?" she heard from the doorway.

When she looked up, she saw Courtney and Jeff

watching her, endearingly anxious expressions on their faces. "It's gorgeous," Brooke answered. "Did you do all this?"

Courtney shook her head. "Nope. Jeff did it." She grinned and nudged him with her elbow.

"Jeff?" *Jeff?*

"Yeah." He shrugged, but looked pleased. "I copied a picture I found on the Internet. It was like decorating the stage for a play. I like doing the behind-the-scenes stuff like that."

"And you do it well." She had to give him that. And she was not going to ask where he got all this stuff or how much money the two of them had spent. She just wasn't. She was, for the first time in years, just going to enjoy herself.

CHASE HAD BEEN INSTRUCTED to bring wine—a red and a champagne. The phone call had amused him because Jeff's exact words were, "You gotta bring champagne cause it's bottled sunshine or something. And when you pick a red wine, make sure it's velvet on the tongue with a finish that evokes the haunting notes of an ancient rumba."

"A rumba and not a tango?"

"No," Jeff answered him seriously. "It's got to be a rumba. I think a tango might taste different, or something."

What food and wine magazine were they reading?

He found he was far more relaxed than he thought he'd be with the prospect of seeing Brooke again and congratulated himself on getting his emotions back under control.

That twinge couldn't have been regret, could it?

SHE COULD *NOT* wear this dress in public. What had she been thinking? It clung. It clung in places Brooke didn't know were clingable. That would be due to the adjust-a-cleavage bra. Brooke had hooked it on max, since she hadn't thought she had all that much to adjust. But it had found something to adjust somewhere and that something was now gently swelling upward and spilling out over the neckline of her dress.

It was a little much—okay a lot—for a family dinner at home. She was in the process of taking off the dress so she could unadjust herself when Courtney squealed, "Brooke!"

She'd probably set something on fire. Brooke hurried toward the kitchen as fast as she could while wearing sandals that set the women's movement back forty years.

"What happened?" she gasped, heading for the pantry and the fire extinguisher.

"Chase will be here any minute and the candles aren't lit," Courtney moaned. "Jeff and I are both stirring something that takes constant stirring and we can't stop—" Courtney had looked up. "Brooke?" Her eyes widened.

Brooke looked down at herself and saw a lot more than she was used to. "Too much?"

"Yowza," Jeff said in an awed voice.

"Keep stirring!" her sister ordered.

"I'm going to go change."

"*No!*" Courtney and Jeff shouted together. "There's no time," Courtney added.

"The candles should be lit for maximum effect," Jeff explained.

"I think Brooke is already *at* maximum effect," Courtney told him.

"That's it. I'm changing."

"Oh, come on, Brooke. You look great. Just like a regular person now."

"Thanks," Brooke said dryly.

"You know what I mean. Jeff tell her she looks great."

"Yowza squared."

Courtney glared at him. It was that glare more than anything that convinced Brooke to wear the dress after all.

"Do you need me to do anything besides light the candles?" she asked.

"Nah. Just sit in there. Chase is supposed to bring some wine for you guys."

"Okay."

Courtney was draining something at the sink. Jeff caught Brooke's eye and mouthed, "Yowza," once more.

Grinning, Brooke went to find the matches.

There must have been a hundred candles in the den. Brooke lit the ones on the fireplace mantel and hearth first, amazed at the way the glow highlighted the lush table.

It looked like the setting for a sheik's seduction.

Moving on, she made her way around the room, enjoying the shadows.

The doorbell rang before she finished lighting the candles on the bookshelves. Brooke flinched and burnt her knuckle.

"I'll get it," she called and sucked on her knuckle as she opened the door.

HE HAD THE WRONG HOUSE. That couldn't possibly be Brooke at the door. Not navy-suit-and-white-underwear Brooke.

"Hi. Come on in." She stepped back, her knuckle in her mouth.

He knew that voice. It *was* Brooke.

Should he say something? Comment on the way she looked? Would she take it the wrong way, which would be the right way?

He followed her into the room unable to look away from her hips as they moved under that shiny red material. "You look...uh, do you have a date?"

She removed her knuckle from her mouth, blew on it and picked up a box of matches. "No." She glanced up at him. "Valentine's Day is coming up. I'm just dressing for the holiday."

Striking a match, she bent down to light a group of candles on a lamp table.

Don't bend down. Chase's mouth had gone dry, which reminded him of the wine he held. "I was told to bring these." He held up the two bottles.

"The kitchen is through there." She gestured over her shoulder with her head, sending her hair swaying. "Courtney and Jeff are back there cooking 'strange, exotic and wonderful things.'"

"I've got the local pizza delivery place programed into my cell phone."

"Good thinking."

Chase had been concentrating so much on trying *not* to concentrate on Brooke, that he hadn't noticed the rest of the room.

Candles flickered all around him. He took in the table and the pillows and the fabric and smiled to himself. Jeff had raided the storage unit that contained the remnants from his mother's el Haibik marriage. Yeah, his father had lost out to a minor Arab prince who had major bucks. Jeff had said their New York apartment had looked like the inside of a tent.

He headed toward the kitchen, hearing the sounds of squabbling. Great. Things were shaping up nicely.

"You can't just slap the stuff on bread," Jeff was saying. "Remember the visual appeal."

"Then you do it." Courtney shoved a bowl of gray goop toward Jeff. "Just when did you get so visual?"

"We're doing a graphics unit in computer science," Jeff answered her seriously. "It's cool." He took a knife and carefully spread the goop on rounds of bread, then added a sprinkle of something on top. "See?"

Courtney studied it, then slapped her hand over her mouth. "It looks like a—" She burst into laughter.

"I know." Jeff grinned.

"You are soooo bad."

So much for the argument. Chase walked on into the kitchen. "Is that bad good, or bad bad?"

Still laughing, they looked up at him. "Oh, good, Chase is here."

"Hey, man. Did you bring the wine?"

Chase held up the bottles. "And the champagne is chilled."

"Great." Jeff continued to work with the goop. "Courtney, can you get the glasses?"

Chase was tempted to tell him not to make very many of the strange-looking appetizers, visual appeal or not.

"We're going to let you handle this." Courtney handed him two champagne flutes with glass stems shaped to form 2000. "I got them for half-price since they were millennium leftovers."

Chase smothered a smile.

"Go sit and talk to Brooke." Courtney shooed him out of the kitchen. "We'll be in with hors d'oeuvres in a minute."

Champagne and a lady in a red dress. Not exactly how Chase had pictured the evening. It shouldn't be this way, but he'd forgotten why.

Brooke was reaching above her head, setting lighted candles on a shelf. Her dress rose as she did so, exposing an expanse of thigh, a thigh he was intimately familiar with.

And the candles...the flickering shadows were sculpting her body beneath that dress. He was chagrined to realize that he hadn't looked at Brooke as a whole until now.

On the whole, it was pretty nice.

She saw him standing there. "How are they doing?"

"Okay. I think."

"Yeah, I know. It doesn't actually smell bad in there, just like it has the potential to turn bad at any second."

Chuckling eased the tightness in his throat. "I've been drafted for champagne duty." He set the glasses and bottle on the table and withdrew the small penknife on his key chain.

"Okay." She stood back and blew out a match. "The first hundred or so candles are lit. I've only got the table and the ones inside the fireplace left."

Chase watched her walk across the room as he cut the foil with his knife, then untwisted the wire holding the cork in place.

Brooke knelt down and he caught his breath, then turned away to remove the cork.

Stop it. He ought to be angry, not aroused. What did she think she was doing by wearing that dress? They'd agreed that any feelings between them were gone, and even though he'd lied, it was only a temporary lie.

But if that's the way she wanted to play, then so be it. He'd been very up front with her about not looking for a relationship and although a superficial encounter wasn't his style, he certainly wasn't going to judge those who had no problems with them—at least those who weren't related to him. Yes, he could be open-minded.

The cork popped hard against his palm as though punctuating his decision. He poured two glasses of a very nice Argentinean sparkling wine and purposefully strode over to the woman who was on her knees lighting candles that emphasized lusher curves than he remembered.

She blew out the last match, her shining lips pursed suggestively. Rocking back on her heels, she gazed around the room and finger-combed her hair back from her face. "Looks great. I shouldn't have bothered to dust."

Chase handed her a glass and joined her on the floor pillows. "What are we drinking to?"

Brooke's glass was already halfway to her mouth. "Oh. To younger brothers and sisters finally seeing reason?"

"I was thinking of something more along the lines of…" He let his gaze drift over her, lingering unmistakably in places worth lingering. "To a woman's perogative to change her mind."

Brooke stared hard at him and didn't drink. "I trust you're referring to Courtney?" She took a cautious sip.

"No." He leveled his gaze at her. "I'm referring to you."

Brooke's glass of champagne thunked to the table, causing a sizzle as a little splashed onto one of the candles.

"Hey." She clicked her fingers in front of his face. "Snap out of it."

He captured her hand and pressed a kiss into the palm.

"Chase!" She jerked her hand away and glanced toward the kitchen. "What are you *doing?*"

"Just responding to all this." He indicated the room and then inched closer to Brooke. "And to you."

"But I don't want you responding to me."

Sure she didn't. He could hear the breathy little quiver she tried to hide. He could see the way she stared at his mouth, then licked her lips.

Most important of all, though, was the fact that she swayed ever so slightly toward him.

Chase leaned forward, brushed her hair off her neck and inhaled deeply.

"No!" She pushed him back so quickly that he nearly spilled his wine.

Setting it on the table next to her glass, he narrowed his eyes at her. "What is this, Brooke? Your way of getting back at me?"

She gave him a withering glance, and so help him, he withered. "This. Isn't. About. You."

"Then explain the dress."

"Oh, for—" Brooke grabbed her champagne and took a long sip. "I was beginning to sound and look more like our mother than she did. Why should Courtney listen to anything I have to say when she thinks I'm so out of it?" She drank more champagne. "And I am out of it. I was dressing old, acting old and sounding old. You'd hardly know that I'm barely seven years older than Courtney. She thinks I work too hard, save everything I make and have no fun. Maybe so, but I'm doing exactly what I want to be doing for now. But Courtney thinks it's horrible and is afraid she'll end up exactly like me."

In his mind, Chase could hear similar words spoken by Jeff.

"So I bought this dress...I guess to show Courtney there is life after twenty—are you paying attention to me?"

"Oh, yes."

"I'm up here. You're looking at my breasts."

"In spite of opinions to the contrary, men can multitask." The smile he gave her didn't contain the slightest hint of apology.

"I should be outraged by that remark."

Chase picked up her glass and handed it to her. "But you're not because you know that you look incredibly hot in that dress. And—fair warning—I plan to enjoy the view." He clinked his glass to hers. "Here's to life after twenty."

Her eyes sparkled in the candlelight and Chase hoped there was life after thirty as well.

"Madame and monsieur." Jeff spoke with a very bad French accent. In fact, to Chase's ears, it sounded more German than French, probably because Jeff was studying German in school.

"For your dining plazeer, ve half zee appetizers." With a flourish, he presented the plate of gray goop hors d'oeuvres and celery sticks.

Chase and Brooke stared at them.

"What do we have here?" Brooke asked gamely.

"Walnut paté and celery sticks."

"Aren't you and Courtney going to have any?" Chase asked.

"Zee chef, she is not feenished." Jeff bowed his way out of the room.

Chase and Brooke stared at the plate. "Is, ah, is walnut paté an old family recipe?"

"Not our family," Brooke said and took a celery stick. "Celery and champagne. Interesting combo."

"I'm going for the walnuts." Chase picked up one of the bread rounds and bit into it. "Not bad. Like peanut butter without the peanuts."

"Walnut butter."

"Walnuts and something else. Try one." He picked up a piece. "It grows on you."

"That's what I'm afraid of."

Chase laughed and when she wouldn't take it, kept moving it toward her mouth until she said, "This better not be as bad as it looks," and bit into it.

"Interesting." But Brooke reached for another celery stick.

Chase ate another walnut thing. If the rest of the food was as weird as this, then he figured he'd better eat what he could stand when he got the opportunity.

He was reaching for another one when Brooke grabbed his wrist. "What?" Her expression was as strange as the food.

"Look."

"Where?"

"At the *plate*."

"Why? Is something crawling on it?"

Brooke took a swallow of her champagne. And then another one. "Look at the arrangement of food."

"Okay. I'm looking." What did she see? He shook his head.

"Two rounds of walnut paté with a celery stalk between them and the pattern is repeated. Suggest anything to you?"

They stared at the plate.

"It suggests that your mind works in intriguing ways." He couldn't be certain, but Chase thought she might have blushed. "I'll get the champagne bottle."

Chase stood and walked over to the table trying to convince himself that they weren't seeing what they were seeing. That it was a perfectly innocent arrangement of food.

"I'm sorry," she said when he returned. "That was inappropriate."

He refilled her glass. "Except now that you've pointed it out, the arrangement does look like, well..."

Neither of them ate anymore.

Shortly Jeff, his accent no better, arrived with another course. "Pine nut zoop," he said, setting the bowls in front of them.

"Pine nut soup?" Brooke repeated, looking puzzled.

"Hey, you didn't finish your walnut paté and celery," he said in his regular voice.

He sounded so disappointed that both Chase and Brooke took more. "We were savoring them," Chase said. "Why don't you and Courtney eat the rest?"

"Uh, okay." Jeff carried away the plate.

Chase picked up a spoon. "I don't believe I've ever had pine nut soup."

"I haven't, either. And if Courtney has, I'd like to know where."

"And why," Chase added. "Want to toss a coin to see who tastes it first?"

"My turn." Brooke dipped her spoon into the thick yellow liquid and tentatively took a sip. She rolled the mouthful around on her tongue. "It's good!" she said in obvious surprise.

Chase needed no further encouragement. "Hey, it is." He thankfully continued to eat.

"So you know what that means," Brooke said.

"What?"

"That it's got about a zillion calories and fat grams. I taste cream."

He looked at her, trying not to notice the way her lips and throat looked as she ate the soup. "But who cares, right?"

"Right." She swallowed, eyes closed. "It feels like velvet going down."

And tasted like liquid sin. Did she have to look like that when she ate it? He was having enough difficulty ignoring his reaction to the dress alone. He couldn't ignore expressions of ecstasy as well.

"I have to admit that I had no idea Courtney could cook like this." She smiled up at him, leaning close to whisper. "I thought she'd panic."

Chase indicated the other two places at the table.

"Speaking of, they *are* planning to eat with us, aren't they?"

"That's what they said."

Good. He needed someone else to dilute Brooke's effect. He didn't know what it was—except for the dress and her expression and just the fact that it was Brooke—but he had to constantly remind himself that pure lust unsullied by a deeper, richer emotional connection was a bad thing. That giving into said lust was a sure way to ruin a relationship, except that because of the lust, he didn't have a relationship to ruin.

It had seemed to make sense at the time. But that was then and this was now.

Brooke scraped her spoon across the bottom of her bowl, licked off the last of the soup, then gave him an impish look that made him forget to breathe.

Watching him, she leaned close and then closer still.

Then she dipped her spoon into his soup and, laughing, stole a mouthful.

He forced himself to smile indulgently. "Do you want the rest of it?"

She shook her head. "It doesn't taste as good if you offer it to me."

"I can make it taste as good."

The light of challenge was in her eyes. "Show me."

She'd said, "Show me." He'd distinctly heard her. "You sure?"

She tossed her hair over her shoulder and nodded.

All righty then. "Come here."

She hesitated, obviously having second thoughts, then scooted her pillow over about an inch and a half.

"Lean closer."

Strictly speaking, she didn't have to lean closer, but the view was so much better when she did. He dipped his finger into the soup and gently drew it across her lower lip.

Surprise flickered through her eyes, but her tongue stole out and licked her lip. "Uhm. I see what you mean. Except a girl could starve that way."

Chase dipped his spoon into the soup, sipped from one side, then offered her the other. For an instant, he didn't think she'd go for it. Then, looking unblinkingly into his eyes, Brooke steadied his hand with her own and sipped from the other side of the spoon.

"How was that?" His voice was a whisper. He hadn't started out that way, but when he couldn't voice the first word, had to keep whispering.

"You're right."

Not about everything, he wanted to tell her, but she backed up and looked toward the kitchen. "Courtney?" she called. "Do you need any help?"

Twin "no's" came from the kitchen and moments later, Jeff appeared again, carrying another platter. Courtney followed, bringing small containers of sauces.

"Didja like the soup?"

"Yes," Brooke said, way too calmly for Chase's ego. "It was fabulous. You're a great cook. Why haven't I known that?"

"'Cause I didn't!" Courtney was clearly pleased with herself.

And then Jeff set the platter in front of them. Chase froze the instant he recognized the contents. Oysters. Raw oysters.

He stared hard at Jeff, who kept his head down as he scuttled back to the kitchen.

"We'll be out with the rest of the meal and we'll finally get to eat!" Courtney practically skipped back to the kitchen.

"Do you..." Chase cleared his throat. "Do you have a thing for oysters on the half shell?"

Brooke's eyes met his. "I take back my apology about the celery and walnut paté."

Nodding, Chase drew a deep breath. "You can have it." And then he added, because someone had to say it, "Apparently, we're being fed aphrodisiacs."

"Chase, I swear, I had no idea. What are they trying to do?"

"Well, obviously—"

"I mean, I *know* what, but why?"

"I have no idea. Should we let on that we know?"

Brooke shook her head. "And we'd better not give them any reason to think it might actually be working. I mean, come *on.*"

With that, Brooke stabbed an oyster, dunked it into a red sauce and defiantly put it in her mouth and swallowed.

"Well, there's nothing seductive about a face like that."

"Oh, ick, oh, ick, oh, ick." She drained the last of her champagne then set the glass down. "Your turn."

"Gladly. I happen to like oysters." Chase picked up an oyster, shell and all, and tilted the contents into his mouth.

If possible, Brooke's expression was even more disgusted than before. "You know, aphrodisiac or not, I just don't think oyster breath is going to work for me."

"If you'll recall, nothing is supposed to be working for you."

"And who said it was?"

Chase stared at her. Unfortunately, everything was working for him.

And he was suffering.

8

"IT'S NOT WORKING! They should be really uncomfortable by now."

"Or all over each other. The man has got to be made of stone. Your sister is *hot*. Wow...I mean *old* guy hot. You know."

"Just get the potatoes out of the oven. I'm going to chop veggies."

BROOKE DISCREETLY moved her pillow as far from Chase as she could, which wasn't far since the coffee table wasn't all that huge. She didn't want Courtney or Jeff to think their clumsy and misguided attempt to get something going between her and Chase was having any success.

And it wasn't. Not much, anyway. Well, other than the way Chase looked at her in that dress. And the way that look made her feel.

She and Chase were in complete agreement. It wasn't enough to base a relationship on physical attraction alone, no matter how strong. It was unfortunate that the timing in their lives didn't permit them to develop a relationship, but he'd been very honest and logical, which was attractive all by itself, if not very flattering.

But she knew he was right as she'd reminded herself continuously—especially during their...polite flirting, she'd call it. Some men would have taken advantage.

Darn it anyway. She sighed and stared at the bottom of her champagne glass.

"Owwww!" A feminine wail reverberated throughout the house. Apparently Courtney's string of luck in the kitchen had ended.

Jeff came running out, flung down two wineglasses and the bottle of red, then panted, "Band-Aids?"

Brooke pointed. "Master bathroom medicine cabinet."

Jeff jogged through the den as Brooke listened for further sounds from the kitchen.

"Did you want to check on your sister?" Chase asked into the silence.

"Yes, but I'm not going to because Courtney would interpret it as hovering."

"Oh, look," Chase said in exaggerated dismay. "No corkscrew. I'll just have to go into the kitchen and find one."

"Thanks," Brooke whispered as Jeff came barreling back through the room.

Within moments Chase had returned with the corkscrew and news that Courtney's cut wasn't deep and the bleeding was under control.

Shortly after that, both Courtney and Jeff carried in the plates and this time, they joined Chase and Brooke.

It was an odd assortment of food, some of which she recognized and some of which she didn't.

"So what do we have here?" Chase asked.

"Well," Courtney pointed with her bandaged finger, "Those are figs, grapes and bananas with dates, then steamed zucchini and carrots, broiled tomatoes and cucumbers. The brown stuff is scrambled eggs with truffles and next to that are new potatoes topped with caviar." She looked extremely pleased with herself. "And there's French bread with an artichoke and pepper pesto dipping sauce."

"What an...interesting combination of foods," Brooke said. "Bread, Chase?"

He tore off a sizable hunk, noticed Courtney watching him expectantly, and dipped a piece into the artichoke sauce.

Only because she was sitting right next to him and looking for any kind of reaction, did Brooke notice his eyelids flicker. Nodding, he swallowed, then reached for his water. "Spicy—but good."

Brooke tore off a piece of bread, but beneath the table, Chase gripped her knee in warning. The strength with which he held on left no doubt that it *was* a warning.

She glanced up at him and noticed that the candlelight reflected the tears that had collected in the corner of his eyes. Merciful heavens, what had Courtney put in that stuff?

Brooke could imagine the comments next to the recipe, "Gets the blood stirring," or something similar.

She looked at her plate. The vegetables looked innocuous, except for the curdled white stuff and inky smears on the potatoes. Brooke stabbed a carrot and it tasted just like a carrot. She gave Courtney a thumbs up and ate some more vegetables, then bananas and grapes.

Chase really was a sweetie for going along with this, but she didn't dare look at him. Jeff and Courtney were staring as though they expected Brooke and Chase to explode with unbridled passion at any moment.

Time for project get-an-education-first to begin.

"Courtney, I'm so impressed, but you'd better watch it, or Jeff will expect a feast like this every night after you're married."

And Chase, bless him, responded to the cue. "But if they eat like this every night, Jeff's trust fund money won't last long."

Wow. Brooke was impressed.

Jeff grinned. "Quit kidding around, Chase."

"You're right, I am exaggerating a little. After all, you'll both be working, so it'll be a nice supplement until you're earning more than minimum wage."

"Courtney's waitressing tips will put her over the minimum wage mark," Brooke reminded him.

"Oh, that's right." Chase nodded solemnly. "On the other hand, when you calculate in their living expenses—"

"You said we could live with you," Jeff pointed out.

"Not unless you're going to school. And even then,

you'll want to get out on your own, and do things your own way. I am pretty set in my routine."

"But besides rent there's the phone, car expenses, insurance, that sort of thing." Brooke looked over at them. "You two have discussed a budget, haven't you?"

"Well...no." Jeff was doing most of the talking. Courtney had gone all quiet.

"It's important that you do so, especially the insurance. What if Courtney's cut had been worse? A trip to the emergency room can cost hundreds of dollars and once she's married, she's off our parents' medical plan."

Jeff and Courtney looked dazed.

"You know, Brooke, it's hard to make a budget when you've never had a chance to do it." Chase reached into his back pocket and withdrew a computer printout. "I knew the subject would come up, so I crunched a few numbers." He handed the paper to Jeff. "That's based on equal quarterly payments from your trust as long as it lasts, and on Courtney making minimum wage, since I'd forgotten about her undoubtedly superior waitressing skills."

"Nice touch," Brooke murmured for his ears alone.

"You drew up a budget for us?"

The look on their faces was priceless.

Chase nodded as Jeff and Courtney put their heads together.

"Hey! My trust fund is bigger than this."

"Yes, but the rules for withdrawal change if you marry prior to age twenty-one."

Jeff's face hardened. "What have you done?"

"Nothing. However, it appears that the el Haibik attorneys have had a lot of experience dealing with young men who have access to large amounts of cash."

"Huh?"

"Your mother left it up to her former husband's attorneys to set up the trust, which, after all, was part of the divorce settlement. As I understand it, there has been an attempt to curb some of the excesses by the young Saudi royalty. Too much bad press. They used their standard forms."

"I am *not* a Saudi prince!"

"But you are eighteen and having been eighteen myself once, I can see their point."

Jeff flung the printout down and Courtney had to rescue it as it drifted toward the votive candles.

"Jeff, this is more than a lot of couples have starting out. If we're careful, we won't have to go into debt."

"What are you *talking* about?" he snapped at her.

Brooke had never heard easygoing Jeff snap at anything. Apparently, neither had Courtney. Her sister blinked and swallowed visibly.

Jeff scowled and pushed the food around on his plate.

Brooke inhaled prior to saying something that would smooth over the situation when she felt a warning tap under the table.

Oh, right. Chase was reminding her that this is what they had hoped would happen. Brooke hadn't realized that it would be so painful to witness.

Courtney had spent so much time and effort on dinner, too. And had Jeff complimented her? Granted, he'd helped, but still.

Brooke took a forkful of the unfortunately brown scrambled eggs. Truffles were expensive, she knew. What had Courtney...

A sickly, eggy, sweet taste filled her mouth. Chase was also preparing to sample the eggs and this time, Brooke was the one to grab *his* knee.

She was going to have to force herself to swallow, preferably without gagging. She made it. Barely, and only because she followed with a huge drink of water and followed that with wine, which probably wasn't such a good idea, but made her not care as much.

"Courtney, what's in the eggs?"

"Nothing much. Just eggs and truffles and a little cream. Why?"

"Uhm..."

Courtney took a forkful and made a face exactly like the one Brooke would have made if she'd been free to do so. "It's awful! What happened? I even used Godiva."

"I thought Godiva made chocolate," Brooke said.

"Yeah—chocolate truffles. There are some left over that I thought we could have later."

Someone was going to have to tell her. "Uh... there's another kind of truffle. It's like a black mushroom. A really expensive mushroom. They hunt them with..."

"Pigs," Chase finished.

"No way," Jeff said.

"Way."

Courtney looked horrified. "I thought the recipe meant chocolate!" Her face crumpled. "I wanted this evening to be perfect! I've worked all day and I haven't had a chance to eat—"

"I love chocolate scrambled eggs!" Chase said with hearty enthusiasm, which was necessary for him to be heard over Courtney's sobs. He demonstrated by eating two quick bites and chewing in a good imitation of bliss.

"When I was a kid, I used to pour syrup on my eggs on Saturday morning. That's when Mom brought me breakfast on a tray in front of the TV while I was watching cartoons." He took another mouthful. "Yeah. Really brings back the memories."

Courtney snuffled. "Really?"

"Oh, man, yeah." As they watched, he ate his entire serving.

What a...sweetie. In the best and most manly sense of the word, if that were possible. It was all Brooke could do to keep from flinging herself at him.

And if he hadn't looked the slightest bit green in the candlelight, she would have.

"JEFF HAS the silliest idea that I won't marry him now that he won't get the money from his trust fund as fast as he thought. I don't know what to do." Courtney eyed Brooke as she loaded the dishwasher. "I feel so awful."

Ever since the dinner, she'd been helping out more in the kitchen. Brooke was putting away groceries.

Normal groceries. "You'll have to convince him that you're serious when you take him 'for or poorer.'"

"I know, but he's really mad. He even called his mom."

"What did she say?"

"Pretty much what Chase said."

"How *do* you feel about it?"

"Like I need to do something really spectacular to let him know I haven't changed my mind."

"Well, hey, Valentine's Day is Monday. The magazines are full of ideas."

"Yeah!" Courtney turned a sunny face to her. "Valentine's Day. The most romantic day of the year. Perfect! Thanks, Brooke!"

Wait a minute—two seconds earlier, Courtney had been in the depths of despair.

What was going on?

"HEY, CHASE, ya gotta minute?" Jeff knocked on the door of Chase's study.

"Sure." Chase flicked on the screen saver so Jeff wouldn't see that he'd been filling out another college application form. It was late in the application season, but he wanted to hedge Jeff's bets.

Dinner had been successful beyond his wildest hopes. Brooke had played her part perfectly—the part about matter-of-factly mentioning practical concerns. And the part about being past the first uncivilized, intense, inexplicable and just plain old raw desire for him—she'd done a pretty good job with that, too. The part where she wasn't supposed to be attractive to him anymore, she hadn't played well at all.

"Chase? If this is a bad time—"

"No. What do you need?"

"Well, you and Brooke offered to help us go apartment hunting and since tomorrow is Saturday, Courtney and I wondered if we could go then."

Apartment hunting? Wait a minute. They weren't supposed to want to go apartment hunting. On the other hand, maybe that would be a good thing. He smiled. "Sure. I'll just do a search grid on properties—"

"Hey, you don't have to go to all that trouble."

"Jeff." Chase swiveled around in his chair. "I'm a commercial property agent. This is what I do for a living."

Jeff blinked, clearly never having thought about what Chase spent his days actually *doing*. "But not apartments."

Okay, maybe he'd been paying a *little* attention.

"No, but I've got connections." Chase swiveled back around. "If there is an apartment out there in your price range, I'll find it. Trust me."

"WELL, *THAT* was an interesting morning." Brooke glared at Chase as he dropped her back at her house after apartment hunting with Courtney and Jeff.

Chase stared straight ahead. No, the morning hadn't gone as expected. "Those were the best of the worst places I could find."

"I believe you. I'm surprised the car wasn't stolen."

"I don't understand why you're mad at me. Do you realize how much time it took to find run-down places that are still habitable? I didn't know they would actually put a deposit down on one of them."

"I'm mad because you didn't stop them!"

He stared at her. "How was I supposed to stop them? Anyway, it would have embarrassed Jeff in front of Courtney."

"*So?*"

"*You* didn't stop them."

"My sister wasn't the one forking over money for an apartment that had 'protection' included in the rent!"

"No, but your sister obviously agreed to live there."

"What choice did she have?"

"She could have said that they should wait to get married until they could afford something better! That was the whole idea of this little exercise."

"Oh, that's just so...so like a man. Making it the woman's fault."

"Come on, Brooke. Whose idea do you think it was to get married in the first place?"

She looked at him, her mouth working, and so help him, all he could think about was kissing her. He didn't want to argue with her, but when they were together, there was this incredibly exhausting tension all the time. He was tired of fighting it. He started to say something to that effect, but with a squeak of outrage, Brooke got out of his car, slammed the door and stormed up her front walk.

Chase gripped the wheel so that he wouldn't follow her. As soon as he trusted himself, he started his car and headed for his office to continue with his usual Saturday routine.

But hours later Chase found that he couldn't get his usual jump on the coming week. He'd worked Saturdays for years, finding that having his schedule already set when Monday rolled around allowed him to beat out the competition sometimes. Often enough that they began working Saturdays, as well, which meant Chase would sneak in the occasional Sunday, too, if he didn't have other plans. And he rarely did. But today, today Brooke invaded his thoughts.

Before he could talk himself out of it, he called her office. She'd said that she had lined up some interviews that afternoon and he figured she was there by now. He had no idea how long interviews took, or how many she'd scheduled. He was just tossing his future to fate.

Fate decreed that Brooke would answer the telephone.

"Hi!" Chase cringed at the too-jovial tone in his voice.

There was a hesitation. "Chase?"

"Yeah. You aren't in the middle of an interview, are you?"

"No. I wouldn't have answered the phone."

"Great." Now what? Her voice was politely reserved. He couldn't believe this was the same woman who had responded so passionately to him.

"Listen—since we're both still working, would you like to meet for dinner and talk about today?"

"What's there to talk about?"

It was an excuse and they both knew it. "Then forget the talk and just have dinner with me."

She hesitated and the hesitation turned into a silence that went on and on. Just before it became uncomfortable, she asked, "Why?"

A flippant, "Why not?" was on the tip of his tongue. "I just wanted to see you," he admitted instead.

"You saw me this morning."

"I want to see you alone."

"And then what?"

His palms were sweating and so help him, his heart hadn't pounded this hard since he'd asked Tracy Stedman to the junior prom. "And then we'll see what happens."

"Chase...what are we both doing right now?"

"Other than talking on the phone? Working."

"That's right. Working. We're both busy people."

"Too busy, I'm thinking."

Her voice hardened. "Do you remember telling me that shallow encounters weren't your style?"

He remembered all too well. "Yes."

"So you also remember telling me that it would take time to build a relationship and that you had plans that didn't include a relationship right now?"

"Yes."

"So you're calling me and I have to wonder why. Clearly it's not for a relationship, so that leaves a good ole shallow encounter. Do you have any idea how insulting that is?"

He'd blown it. Big time. "I didn't mean to insult you. I just can't stop thinking about you and I...wanted to get together."

"Tell you what. Don't call me until you decide I'm worth your precious time. Because, let me tell you, I am. But men who take too long to figure it out aren't worth mine."

9

"I WAS HOPING we wouldn't have to do this."

"Jeff, Valentine's Day is *tomorrow* and I'm no closer to getting Brooke to okay my film school deposit than I was before."

"I could lend you the money."

"That's so sweet, but you put it down on that awful apartment."

"Oh, yeah. I'm going to get it back."

"Not for thirty days—you heard that guy. No, we don't have any choice now. They need a real good scare. We talked about this. You know what to do."

"You think it'll work?"

"It's Valentine's Day—yeah, it'll work."

"Well, uh, if it doesn't, I think I want to go to the University of Northern Los Angeles. You could go there, too."

"What? Why?"

"Because, well, it's got a good technical film program and I like all that backstage stuff and the special effects. But it's a college, too, and, well, maybe your sister will go for the compromise. I've got some catalogs. Want me to bring them tomorrow?"

"Yeah. We'll have a lot of time on our hands."

BROOKE TOLD HERSELF she'd done the right thing. She wasn't happy about doing the right thing. Doing the wrong thing would have felt so much better. Would it have been so very wrong just to—

Yes. Yes, yes and yes.

The Chase Davenports of the world, with their hot kisses and their lovely hands and their sparing of young men's and women's feelings, had to learn that they couldn't have it both ways.

If Brooke wanted to, she could work herself into quite a snit by thinking along the lines of how Chase thought she was good enough to have a no-strings fling, but not worth the effort to build a meaningful connection—but there were plenty of other things to have snits about. Say the fact that she was making connections all on her own every time she saw or talked with him. It didn't seem to matter whether they were arguing or flirting or just talking. She was connecting. And that each and every damned connection screamed, "He's The One!"

She didn't want him to be The One. She didn't have time.

But you could make time.

And it didn't help her peace of mind to know that she would if he'd only bother to ask.

Brooke groaned. Her head hurt.

On Sunday, Courtney made countless whispered phone calls to Jeff, quickly hanging up when Brooke came into the room.

And she did laundry with a vengeance. Not just the

clothes she needed for immediate wearing, but loads of laundry.

"So, what did you get Jeff for Valentine's Day?" Brooke asked her at one point.

"Oh! That's right, Valentine's Day is tomorrow." Courtney looked distracted.

"I thought you were going to do something extravagant." Not that Brooke meant to encourage extravagance, but she was interested to see if the apartment outing prompted any new developments. Or undevelopments.

"Yeah. I—I was."

And right then, Courtney stopped folding her underwear, grabbed her purse and announced that she was going to the mall.

Hmm. Courtney hadn't bought anything for Jeff for Valentine's Day? Well, well, well.

Things were looking up.

Brooke reached for the phone to call Chase, but stopped herself just in time. Things weren't looking up *that* much.

JEFF HAD BEEN in his room all day, coming out only for their Sunday lunch at the local cafeteria.

It wasn't unusual for Jeff to hole up in his room but after yesterday, Chase had thought he'd want to see Courtney. A couple of times when Chase just happened to be in the vicinity of Jeff's bedroom door, he'd heard the low murmur of a one-sided conversation and realized Jeff was on the phone. Other times, Chase could hear him moving around. A lot.

They hadn't spoken at all about the apartment. It was a tricky subject and Chase didn't want to overdo it.

Nothing that Jeff had done would be considered suspicious. Except that Chase just had a feeling....

He knocked on Jeff's door and heard scrambling.

"Just a sec."

It was more than a "sec" before Jeff opened the door. "Hey."

Chase tried to see past him without Jeff knowing, an impossible feat. "Pizza for dinner?"

"Yeah, sure."

"Pepperoni? The works?"

Jeff wrinkled his forehead as though he were distracted and had to concentrate. "Uh, pepperoni, double cheese."

"Large?"

"Nah. Medium."

"I'll call."

"'Kay." And he shut the door.

Thoughtfully, Chase wandered back down the stairs of his town house. A *medium* pizza. Something was going on.

He went into the kitchen where the pizza coupon files were kept, but when he reached for the phone, it was to call Brooke and see what her take was.

Then he stopped.

He shouldn't call Brooke unless it was for something specific. She'd been very clear and very justified.

And he'd been very...conflicted.

He *had* said one thing, then done another. The thing was, there was no reason for them not to date and get to know each other. Except that he felt as though he *did* know her. That was the problem. He just didn't think he could stand to be around her and casually date, that's all. And this attraction between them was like a raging fire that needed lots of fuel or it would quickly burn itself out. Chase didn't want it to burn out—not that way. He'd seen it happen with his father.

During the days between the dinner and the apartment hunt, he and Brooke had talked frequently. They'd always started out talking about Jeff and Courtney, but there had been times when they'd veered off onto their own subjects.

He...liked her. There was a lot of potential with Brooke. He just didn't know how to tap into it.

TODAY WAS Valentine's Day, as Chase was reminded when Jeff came into the bathroom while he was shaving. "Hey bro, can you hook me up with next quarter's allowance?"

Chase almost cut himself. "For an engagement ring?"

Jeff blinked at him. "Uh, no. It's Valentine's Day, man."

"And you haven't bought anything for Courtney, yet?"

Jeff sheepishly bowed his head.

"I don't have that much cash on me. Can you wait

until after school so I can go by the bank during lunch?"

"Uh, not really."

Chase could understand that. "Then you'll have to make do with the cash I've got in my wallet. Leave me five bucks for a sandwich."

"Thanks." Jeff stood there a moment longer. "You know, I, uh, appreciate you letting me live here with you. I mean, considering you're not even related to me anymore."

"Not a problem." Chase met his eyes in the mirror. "I've enjoyed it." And he had.

"Later, dude." Jeff slapped the doorjamb and left.

Chase thought about the exchange while he finished shaving. It wasn't that he *wanted* to feel suspicious.

But he did.

THAT MORNING, Courtney did the unthinkable. Breakfast. She brewed coffee and put out heart-shaped muffins that she'd bought at the store.

"Happy Valentine's Day, Brooke," she said when Brooke, lured by the smell of coffee, stumbled into the kitchen before her shower.

"Wow." Brooke raked her hair out of her face and grinned when she saw the red mug with a white heart that had the words "my favorite sister" written on it.

"Thanks, Courtney." Brooke filled the mug with coffee.

"I realize you're my *only* sister, but I just wanted

you to know that I appreciate you being here for me while Mom and Dad are in El Bahar. I've probably gotten in the way of you..." She shrugged. "You know, you and guys."

On her way to the refrigerator for milk, Brooke made a detour and hugged her sister. "Come on. You haven't been in the way of anything. We've been just like roomies."

"Still."

Well, it *was* nice to be appreciated. Brooke tilted her head. "You're growing up, aren't you?"

"'bout time, huh?" Courtney smiled and finished the last of her muffin as Brooke poured milk into her coffee.

A honk sounded from the driveway. "That'll be Jeff." Courtney dusted crumbs off her hands and grabbed her backpack.

Brooke pushed aside the miniblinds and saw the Porsche outside. "He's early, isn't he?"

"Uhm, we've got a play...thing before school. Bye!" And she was out the door before Brooke could question her. Did that mean she didn't have rehearsal after school today?

Oh, well. She and Jeff would probably go out to dinner anyway.

Brooke studied her mug, feeling a warmth in her heart that matched the warmth against her hand. Then she went to take her shower.

THE CALL CAME about eleven forty-five, just as Brooke was leaving for lunch.

"This is the West Houston High automated attendance computer. Your child...Courtney...Weathers... has been reported absent from one or more class periods. If you are unaware of this absence, please call the attendance office. As a reminder, to be excused, all absences must be explained in a note. Failure to do so will result in an unexcused absence which will impact..."

The computer droned on, but Brooke had stopped listening. *Courtney hadn't made it to school.* Had she and Jeff had an accident?

With shaking fingers, Brooke copied down the number the computer gave at the end of its speech, and called the school.

They confirmed her worst fear. Brooke made them call the classroom where Courtney was supposed to be, and she wasn't there. Next, she asked to speak with the drama teacher, who was at lunch.

Brooke didn't go to lunch, but that was fine, since she'd lost her appetite. She stayed in her office waiting for the return call, trying not to panic, but panicking anyway.

She'd phoned three hospitals before the drama teacher returned her call, telling Brooke that there had been no early-morning rehearsal.

Trying not to hyperventilate, she called Chase.

His voice mail answered, saying that he had gone to San Antonio for the day.

Oh, great. Just great. Fabulous.

Brooke left a message asking him to call her, in case

he was the obsessive type who constantly checked his voice mail.

San Antonio was a several-hour drive away. Brooke was going to have to handle this situation by herself.

Calling the school back, she asked if Jeff Ryan was also absent. Though they didn't want to discuss another student with her, she allowed a bit of hysteria to sound in her voice and came away with the information that Jeff was also absent.

With a sinking feeling, Brooke remembered the breakfast Courtney had fixed, the gift of the mug and the thank-you speech.

It had sounded like she was saying goodbye.

What had those two done?

Brooke had no intention of sitting in her office worrying, so she took the afternoon off and headed for home.

Once there, she ran into Courtney's room.

Clothes were scattered everywhere and the closet doors stood open. There was a gaping hole where her suitcase had been.

Brooke pawed through the mess on Courtney's unmade bed, looking for a note—anything.

When she found nothing, she went over to Courtney's desk and searched through the papers and teenage debris. She had never invaded Courtney's privacy before.

She found old homework papers and various school stuff, along with doodlings saying, "Mrs. Jeff Ryan" and "Courtney Ryan." There was a brochure for the Los Angeles Film School and an application that was partially completed.

And then there was the paper with numbers and the word Continental encircled with hearts. The airline?

Following a hunch, Brooke called the airline and asked if the numbers she'd found were flight numbers.

They were—for flights to Las Vegas.

Las Vegas. Valentine's Day. Deposit on an apartment. Absent from school. It didn't take a genius to connect the dots. And the dots led straight to an elopement.

Brooke sank onto Courtney's bed. How could she be so stupid?

Jeff has the silliest idea that I won't marry him now that he won't get the money from his trust fund as fast. I need to do something really spectacular to let him know I haven't changed my mind.

Well, eloping to Las Vegas on Valentine's Day was spectacular, Brooke had to give her sister that.

She went back to the desk and found computer printouts hidden—but not very well—of wedding chapel Web sites. "Courtney, you idiot!"

Time to call Chase again. She left another voice mail telling him everything she'd discovered so far, along with the names of the chapels. One in particular, Doves and Diamonds, had markings next to it— little doodles of doves and diamonds—and Brooke felt that must be the one the kids had chosen.

The voice mail timed out on her, and she had to call back with part two of the message.

This was one of those times when she wished she had a cell phone. She couldn't wait around here for Chase to call and she had to do something. A thought occurred to her. It was Valentine's Day after all, and probably a busy time for the wedding chapel business. Maybe Courtney and Jeff would be delayed long enough, say, for a sister to talk them out of getting married.

Brooke gathered all the papers she'd found, changed her clothes, put on walking shoes and headed for the airport.

CHASE HAD EXCUSED himself from the lunch table to give his clients time to discuss the properties he'd shown them. One, in particular, was perfect and they were intelligent enough to realize it. All he had to do was sit back and wait for the offer.

It would be a sweet deal. He had enough negotiating latitude to make a good profit for the company, good enough to put him in bonus territory, along with a tidy commission for himself.

A very tidy commission. If he didn't lose his head and do something frivolous like buy a new car, he could invest the entire amount and maybe accelerate his timetable for settling down a bit.

The bulk of the San Antonio lunch hour crowd had gone back to work. Chase settled on a bar stool in the lounge area and called in to his office. He had taken notes on two messages, when a mechanical voice announced that Jeff wasn't in school. The next message was a near-hysterical one from Brooke. No, that wasn't fair, it was only urgent sounding, but it could have been near-hysterical and he would have felt it completely appropriate, considering what she had to say.

So Courtney wasn't at school, either.

The next message from Brooke was even more ominous.

"They eloped?" Chase shouted aloud. He replayed the message, listening incredulously to what Brooke had discovered. As he took notes, he remembered the odd conversation with Jeff this morning. He'd been saying goodbye.

When he'd listened to both parts of Brooke's message again, Chase clicked off and fought the urge to order a schooner-sized margarita.

Jeff was being an idiot. Well, like mother, like son.

Chase called back into his office and discovered that another message had been left—Brooke was calling from the airport telling him that she was leaving for Vegas and would he please give her his cell number.

How was he supposed to do that?

And what did she think she was going to accomplish by flying to Las Vegas?

Without him?

Chase called his building switchboard operator. "Lila, could you please intercept my calls? If Brooke Weathers phones, please give her my cell number."

And now...Chase drew a deep breath. He was going to have to extricate himself from the two gentlemen he'd left at the table.

He walked back, briskly, purposefully and confidently, sat down, put his forearms on the table and leaned forward. "Gentlemen, have you come to a decision?"

They regarded him carefully, as aware as Chase was that he'd skipped a step—or several—in the negotiating process.

"We're certainly considering the properties you've shown us—"

"And have decided the one at 24 Industrial is perfect, am I right?"

They chuckled. Warily.

"So, let's wrap this up." Chase got out his calculator, cut out all his bonus profit, slashed his commission and said, "Three point eight five mil."

Neither man said a word. They were, no doubt, in shock. Frankly, so was Chase. He was going to have to do some fast talking or they'd think he'd just learned something that would devalue the property.

"I'm pretty sure I could get four and a quarter, maybe four fifteen. Certainly four. But I want to sell it to you and I want to sell it now. Why, you wonder." Chase shook his head as he put his calculator away. "Because, I need to fly to Vegas to stop my eighteen-year-old stepbrother from eloping in order to get at his trust fund."

The younger of the two men began the standard response to Chase's unstandard offer, "You've certainly given us something to think about—"

"Deal," said the older man.

The younger man actually gasped. "Dex, you shouldn't—"

Dex waved him silent. "The man's buying time, son. Watch and you may learn something."

JUST BEFORE Brooke got off the plane, a flight attendant handed her a message slip with the words "Chase Davenport" and a phone number.

Inexplicably, she felt lighter, as though she were closer to finding Courtney and Jeff.

Clutching the paper, she went in search of a telephone.

He answered almost immediately. "Brooke?"

Relief coursed through her. "Am I glad to hear your voice. Where are you?"

"Still in San Antonio waiting for a flight."

"You don't have to come." But she hoped he would.

"Yeah, I do," he said matter-of-factly.

It was a throwaway comment—or it would have been to anyone else. But to Brooke, Chase's very simple declaration told her a lot about the man he was.

He honored his commitments. Jeff, who wasn't even related to him, was eighteen, and legally could do almost anything he wanted. No one would blame Chase for letting him do just that. But Chase had agreed to watch out for his former stepbrother and that was what he was going to do.

He'd also agreed to work with Brooke, and he was honoring that commitment as well.

There was absolutely no resentment in his voice. Concern, yes. Frustration, yes. Weariness, kinda. Determination—you bet.

At that moment, Brooke had one of those rare, clear insights into the future and saw what kind of life partner Chase would make.

It made her break out in a cold sweat because she wanted that future so very, very much.

Unaware of her thoughts, Chase had continued to speak in a rapid recitation of facts. "I had a friend drive by my town house and Jeff wasn't there. He went by your house, too, and there weren't any cars in the driveway either. I called Jeff's relatives out there—"

"Jeff's got relatives in Vegas?" This was looking bad.

"Jeff's got relatives everywhere."

"So you agree they might actually be headed to Las Vegas? You don't think I jumped to conclusions?"

"No. Now tell me what you've got."

So Brooke went over the notes on chapels she'd found.

"I can't believe they're doing this," Chase said. "Why now? It makes no sense."

"It must to them," Brooke replied, sick of trying to figure out her sister. "Listen, I want to get a start in finding them. I'll keep in touch, okay?"

"Just a minute." There was a muffled conversation and an "I'll take it." Chase spoke into the phone. "They've got me on a flight that leaves in fifteen minutes with a stop in El Paso and Phoenix."

"Oh, poor you."

"Yeah, but I'll get there. Hang on."

"Okay. See you at the airport." And it was scary how much she was looking forward to it.

BROOKE RENTED A CAR. Of course, it wasn't as easy as that. First, she had to put a serious dent in her already dented credit card. Then there was the fact that she hadn't prereserved a vehicle.

What was prereserved? She could understand reserved, but prereserved? Apparently the "pre" was important enough that she should figure it out when she had time. For now, it meant a wait. Brooke didn't want to wait, but she didn't want to spend hundreds of dollars on a luxury car, either.

There appeared to be a car shortage because of the popularity of Valentine's Day in Las Vegas.

She ended up signing a waiver and agreeing to take the next available car before it could be inspected and prepped for rental.

The next available one was a dusty blue compact previously driven by an older couple, which made Brooke feel reassured. At least they wouldn't have been drag racing on the strip. She got in and took off, having already studied the map while she waited.

The Dove and Diamonds Wedding Chapel was a white building with an archway adorned with sparkling silver doves.

The parking lot was full.

Brooke parked on the street in the "limos only" space and ran inside.

And was hit with the glory that was a Las Vegas wedding chapel. Her first impression was of silver, then white. Lots of silver and white.

Anxious and/or kissing couples waited on white sofas in the anteroom. Beyond the double doors, Brooke could see a wedding in progress. She didn't recognize the bride or the groom, and Courtney and Jeff weren't among those waiting.

Brooke felt a peculiar sensation of relief, mixed with disappointment. Either she'd missed the wedding or they'd chosen another chapel.

A persistent throaty cooing mingled with the hushed murmuring. White doves in white wrought-iron cages hung from the ceiling and balanced on pedestals, but only the ones by the chapel doors were real. The rest were mechanical. The sounds Brooke heard were from a dove sound track.

Funny, she'd never pictured Courtney as a dove person. Maybe she'd seen this place in person and changed her mind.

A woman in a silver dress that cried out for a magic wand approached Brooke.

"Party?"

"No, thanks," Brooke said.

"The name of your party?" she clarified, her ethereal expression unchanged.

"Weathers? Or Ryan?"

The woman scanned the waiting couples, then gestured for Brooke to follow her. She stopped at a white podium that supported a huge silver-and-white guest book and feathered pen. Running a finger down the pages, she shook her head.

"I don't see either a Weathers or a Ryan. There's one more place we can look." She beckoned Brooke over to a discreet alcove behind a screen.

The woman sat behind a desk, moved a plastic display sign that said, Ask About Our Valentine Special, and accessed her computer. She typed in one name, stared at the screen and shook her head, then typed in the other name. "They haven't reserved a time today."

"Could they have just, you know, walked in?"

"On Valentine's Day?" The woman gave a tinkling laugh. "We've been solidly booked for weeks. They would be able to get in only if there had been a cancellation."

"Do you remember if a couple—a young couple— came in here today? I know you see hundreds of couples," Brooke added when the woman gave her a sympathetic look. "But they would have been here maybe around ten or eleven o'clock?"

"I'm sorry," the woman said. "There's the Denim and Diamonds Western Wedding Chapel. Sometimes people get us confused."

"That's probably it," Brooke said, though she didn't believe it for a second. Courtney was even less Western than she was dove.

"Would you like their card?"

Brooke thanked the woman, and took the card. "You've been really kind."

"Not at all. Weddings are a very special occasion in

people's lives. I'll tell you a secret—if you just keep telling yourself that love is at the bottom of it all, the little glitches won't bother you."

It was a lovely sentiment, however, Brooke felt that not being able to find the bride and groom was a glitch that was going to bother her no matter how nice this woman was.

Music swelled suddenly. "Oh, hurry!" The silver woman moved faster than Brooke expected, given the confines of her dress.

Brooke followed in time to be thrust into service distributing handfuls of silver and white feathers and petals from a basket to the waiting couples.

"Everyone over here!" directed the woman just seconds before the double doors swung open and the bride and groom emerged.

Even Brooke threw a handful. And, she had to admit, it was a great effect, if a person went in for that sort of thing, which she didn't.

The instant the bride and groom were out the door, white-coated staff appeared with vacuum cleaners and swept up the remains of the wedding.

"Campbell-Bernstein?" the woman called.

Brooke set down her white wicker basket and left.

Once she got out to her car, thankfully not towed or blocked by a limo, she tried not to dwell on the fact that she hadn't found the runaways and studied the remaining chapel printouts.

Chapel of Bliss looked the most promising, especially since it specialized in "weddings for the budget traditionalist."

The Chapel of Bliss was a white building with an archway adorned with flowers, bells and bows.

The parking lot was full.

Brooke parked on the street in the "limos only" space and ran inside.

She could immediately see the budget aspect of the chapel. There was just one room, largish though it was. A ceremony was in progress at the far end. Other wedding parties occupied the pews and maintained a respectable semisilence. Brooke saw everything from jeans to formal gowns, complete with train and veil.

A sign to her left instructed couples to sign in and be seated, reminding them to give the same courtesy to others that they would want for themselves.

Against the wall was a bulletin board with three selections of artificial bridal bouquets, boutonnieres, music cassettes and coupons for discounts at various hotels. A brochure explained various photography and video packages that were available.

Brooke edged over to the ornate scheduling book and checked the names, but didn't see Courtney's or Jeff's. She flipped through the pages and didn't see anything for tomorrow or the day after, either.

Quietly, she left just as the minister turned on the tape recorder and the strains of "We've Only Just Begun" accompanied the newlyweds' first kiss.

Brooke stopped off at a fast-food place for a large iced tea and to use the phone and track Chase's progress.

He was already in Phoenix.

"Haven't found them?"

"No, but I've only managed to check out two places."

"Wouldn't it be easier to make a few calls?"

"I don't think the chapel people will answer the phone today. The chapels are completely booked."

Chase exhaled. "I know. Valentine's Day."

"I'm going to check on a couple more, then I'll pick you up at the airport."

"Brooke? Have you thought about what you're going to say to Jeff and Courtney when you do find them?"

"No."

"Just...if they're already married, go easy on them."

"Why, Chase, you old softie."

"No, but...let's just say I know firsthand that once something is said, it can't be unsaid. And, you know, she's your sister, no matter what she does."

"I know. But thanks for reminding me."

10

"So, WHAT DO YOU think of the brochure?"

"Hey, you know, this University of Northern Los Angeles isn't bad. There are some awesome courses."

"Toldja."

BROOKE STRUCK OUT at the Chapel by the Hill, the Gazebo in the Park and the Chapel of the Crystal Bell before heading for the airport. She had decided to let Chase experience the Elvis-themed chapels with her. Call it her Valentine's gift to him.

She was a little early, or his plane was a little late. Whatever. It didn't matter as soon as she saw him get off the plane. Her heart beat faster and there was a telltale fluttering in her stomach that might have been hunger, but she didn't think so.

He came right up to her and enveloped her in a great hug.

"How did you know I needed a hug?" she murmured against his chest.

A rumbling chuckle vibrated against her cheek. "Because I did, too."

They pulled apart and he looked down at her. "To hell with it," he said. "I'm going to kiss you."

And he did, right there in the middle of the crowd

of people coming and going on the most romantic day of the year.

It had been too long since he'd kissed her. Brooke leaned into the kiss, not caring how it looked either to Chase or anyone else at the airport. She didn't care.

As always, the effect of kissing Chase hit her full force. There was never any halfway response with him. Just wham! and she was ready to empty her bank account to join the airport first-class lounge so they could get horizontal. Or vertical. And naked. In private. Or even semiprivate.

With a great wrenching and absolutely no help from her, Chase broke the kiss, inhaled deeply just below her ear in that way he had that gave her femininity an extra tweak and set her from him.

"How did you know I needed a kiss?" she murmured, trying to let him know she could use another. And another.

His lips, the very same lips that had been pressed against hers, curved gently upward. "Because *I* did."

Oh, wow.

They went to find Brooke's rental car, by silent and mutual consent not discussing what had just happened between them until Brooke couldn't stand it.

"It was just a kiss," she said before starting the car.

"Yeah," Chase agreed. "Just a kiss."

He didn't have to agree. "But a nice kiss."

"Umm. Very nice."

"Possibly even great—considering."

"Considering."

"Stop agreeing with me!"

"Okay, it was a totally hot, sexy kiss that not only broke all the rules but made me forget where I was to the point of very nearly flinging you to the floor and ripping off your clothes."

All right then. Brooke gave him a sidelong glance. "Gee. At least I was ready to go hunting for the first-class lounge."

"Would have taken too long." Chase looked out the window and abruptly changed the subject. "I called Jeff's relatives again and they haven't seen the kids."

Changing the subject. Good idea. "I'm not surprised. Courtney and Jeff have got to realize that we're looking for them by now."

"But they might not be expecting us to be looking in Las Vegas."

Brooke thought about that as she pulled into the limo reserved spot in front of the True Blue Elvis Chapel, which was not white, but pale blue. It had no archway, but it did have a blue gazebo.

"You're parked in a reserved spot," Chase pointed out.

"The parking lot is full, just the way every other parking lot has been full today." Brooke got out and slammed the door. "Prepare to be amazed."

But even Brooke, who had seen a lot of amazing stuff that day, was impressed by the over-the-top tribute to the...*blue* period Elvis.

They walked into blue. There was no other way to describe it. Everything from walls to carpet, drapes and chairs was a sapphire blue.

All the staff, both male and female, were dressed à la Elvis in his Vegas glory days—white spangled suit with blue shirt and blue suede shoes.

Having become familiar with the basic chapel layout, Brooke led him over to the scheduling area and they got in line behind another couple, already dressed as Elvis and Priscilla.

"Ya got your basic Blue Hawaii for twelve ninety-five. It can go up from there." The man even spoke in an Elvis accent. "Now if you're lookin' to spend less, we also have Blue Christmas, G.I. Blues, Blueberry Hill, Indescribably Blue and When My Blue Moon Turns Gold Again." He handed them a price sheet and a photo album with pictures of past weddings. "And I'd like to remind you that each and every wedding comes with complimentary limousine transportation to your hotel in Las Vegas's one and only powder-blue limo."

"Want to go move your car?" Chase murmured. "I sense the impending arrival of a blue limo."

She probably ought to, though where she was going to move it, she didn't know. "Why don't you ask if Courtney and Jeff have been here, or are scheduled to be here and I'll wait in the car."

"Gotcha."

Brooke arrived at her car at the same moment the blue limo pulled up and honked the first few bars of "You Ain't Nothin' but a Hound Dog." Repeatedly.

"All right, I'm moving!" Brooke shouted at the driver. "And that's not a blue song," she added as she got in her car, which *was* blue, she hoped he noticed, and drove around the block.

Chase was waiting for her when she got back. The limo was gone.

"They haven't been here, have they?"

He shook his head. "Want me to drive?"

"You know, I think I would." Brooke was tired of driving. She was tired, period.

"Where to?" Chase asked after they switched places.

Brooke sighed. "That was the last of the Web sites and I have a feeling that they took the printout of the one they planned to go to with them."

Chase tapped his fingers on the steering wheel. It looked like a rhythm Brooke had recently heard honked. "Let's get some burgers and think this thing through."

He pulled a breathtaking U-turn and headed for a fast-food drive-through.

Instead of eating inside, they parked and ate in the car with the windows rolled down. They talked, but not about the errant teenagers. They talked about stuff. Important stuff. And they laughed. A lot.

They ignored the awareness simmering beneath the surface.

And Brooke had never enjoyed a dinner more.

Dusk had fallen and the neon signs were ablaze when Chase suggested they continue their search. He pulled out some brochures as Brooke stuffed their trash into the bags and took them to the outside Dumpster.

When she got back to the car, Chase was on his phone. "Thanks. I appreciate it." He showed Brooke the Las Vegas information packet he'd picked up at the Blue Elvis place. Inside, among hotels and restaurants, was a list of chapels. "We might as well start calling. At least we can eliminate the ones that actually answer the phone."

Brooke nodded, leaned her head back on the car seat and listened to Chase try to charm information out of busy chapel personnel. He was batting about fifty-fifty, when she heard his voice change.

"You did?"

Brooke sat up.

"Ryan—young couple—eight o'clock?"

"Which one?" Brooke asked, but Chase held up a hand to quiet her.

"Yes. Thanks." Chase disconnected the call. "I think we've found them."

"Where?"

He showed her the listing.

"The Chapel of Everlasting Love? That sounds like Courtney."

"A J. Ryan has booked the three-rose traditional package for eight o'clock."

"It's almost seven-thirty now."

"I know, so let's get going. Chase started the car. Or tried to. It cranked okay, but didn't want to catch.

"It's not out of gas, is it?" Brooke had thought there was about half a tank left.

He checked the gauge. "No." Fortunately, the engine caught just then. "It's been started and stopped a lot today. Probably got a little vapor lock going on." He pulled out of the fast-food parking lot.

Since Brooke had absolutely no knowledge of cars other than basic maintenance, she just hoped the thing would get them to the next chapel.

It did.

The Chapel of Everlasting Love was a charming white building with a tasteful, unadorned archway. It was lit with beautiful landscaping floodlights instead of the neon favored by most of the buildings they'd passed on the way here.

And there was room in the parking lot.

"It's so pretty! If Courtney is bound and determined to elope, I'm glad she picked this place."

Chase laughed, sobered, then laughed again.

"What's so funny?"

"Women. And you in particular."

"Why?"

"After going to all this trouble to stop the wedding, you see this place and sound like you're ready to walk her down the aisle."

"Walk her down the aisle." Brooke swallowed against a sudden lump in her throat.

"Hey, what's wrong?"

Might as well tell him. "It's just—Mom and Dad aren't here. I hope Courtney isn't eloping because she doesn't want them to spend the money to come home an extra time."

"They wouldn't mind, would they?"

"Of course not! But she's so young. I know they

wouldn't be happy about her giving up school."
Yeah, two daughters who screwed up.

"You realize that she and Jeff can still go to school
if they want to."

"Except she's never wanted to go—at least, not to a
traditional college."

"But she does want to study somewhere. I honestly
don't think Jeff has given a thought to what he'll be
doing after graduation." Chase mustered a smile.
"Shall we go in or sit out here and depress ourselves
some more?"

Brooke mustered a smile right back at him. "Let's
go in."

The interior of the chapel was as charming as the
exterior, though that may have been the effect of the
hour and the candlelight. Plastic and cheap silk flowers didn't look very romantic in the harsh light of
day.

There was an office where business could be con-
ducted out of sight of the waiting wedding parties,
and the chapel doors had just two small heart-shaped
windows so that the ongoing weddings could have
privacy.

Chase knocked on the open office door and a
woman in a red business suit—maybe for Valentine's
Day and maybe not—gestured for them to enter.

"We called about the Ryan wedding," he said.

She consulted her schedule. "Yes. J. Ryan at eight
o'clock. Have they arrived?"

"Not yet," Brooke answered.

She stood. "Let me show you to the bridal dressing area so you can freshen up."

A subtle way of telling them they looked like they'd been traveling all day long, which they had.

Brooke did feel better after touching up her makeup, combing her hair and popping a couple of breath mints. She'd expected Courtney to come through the door at any moment, but there were still fifteen minutes before the wedding, and Courtney had never been known for her punctuality.

Brooke looked outside the room to find Chase pacing. No sign of Courtney and Jeff yet.

When he saw her, he gestured for her to join him on one of the sofas. "I've never been involved in a wedding intervention. Any ideas what we're going to say?"

"How about 'how could you be so stupid?'"

"Maybe not."

"Then I have no more ideas."

Chase gave an unwilling laugh and rubbed his fingers over his eyes. "We should stay calm."

"I'm very calm. Don't I look calm?"

SHE LOOKED like she was about to blow. "Yes, but it looks like the calm before the storm."

Chase didn't know how he felt, now that he was minutes away from confronting Jeff.

He had a feeling eloping had been Courtney's idea, but he wasn't about to say so and get Brooke mad at him. They needed to stick together on this. "We should find out why they felt the need to elope in the first place. Maybe circumstances have changed."

Brooke glared at him. "She's not pregnant. I know this for a fact and do not ask me to give you the details of how I know."

"Okay." He held up his hands palms outward. "Backing off on the pregnancy issue."

"But you're right. We should find out why now."

"And I'd like to hear their long-term plans for after the wedding. I want to know if they've discussed their life's vision, if you will, with each other. You say Courtney wants to act. Most aspiring actresses head for Los Angeles or New York at some point. What does Jeff think about moving?"

They had a productive and rational conversation, barely noticing that it had been some time since the other wedding had ended when the outer door burst open and a youthful couple carrying a garment bag hurried in and ran toward the office. "Are we too late? Her dress wasn't ready..."

"There's plenty of time," Chase heard the woman in the red suit answer. "Just relax and get changed. We're still preparing the chapel."

Moments later, the woman led the two young people past the couch where Chase was sitting with Brooke to the bridal dressing rooms.

"I have a bad feeling about this," Chase said.

Brooke sighed. "But what are the chances of two Jeff Ryans getting married today in Las Vegas?"

"It's not such an unusual name." As he spoke he saw the chapel woman coming toward them.

"They finally made it," she said with a smile.

"That's the eight o'clock wedding?" Brooke asked with resignation.

"Yes," the woman confirmed. "Isn't that your party?"

Chase and Brooke stood. "Wrong Jeff Ryan."

"Oh, dear!" The woman looked genuinely distressed. "Did I say *Jeff* Ryan? The young man's name is Jay."

Chase asked, "When you said Jay, you meant Jay as in J-a-y?"

She nodded.

"My mistake. I thought it was an initial." He could feel Brooke's disappointment. Hell, he might break out into tears, himself.

They left and sat in the car, staring at the bright lights of Las Vegas.

"I'm sorry," Chase said at last.

"It's not your fault. I would have made the same assumption."

But she hadn't. He had. "What do you want to do now?"

"Las Vegas Boulevard is chapel row. Let's go from one end to the other. If we don't find them or evidence that they've been there, then we call it quits."

"Sounds like a plan." Chase turned the ignition. As before, he had to nurse the starter along and by the time the engine caught, the battery didn't sound too great.

But it did catch and that was all that counted.

Las Vegas Boulevard was packed. Dozens of couples had chosen Valentine's Day to get married.

Chase and Brooke went from chapel to chapel without luck. Personally, he'd given up back at the Everlasting Love place, but he knew how Brooke felt. With the chapels so busy, there was a chance—albeit a slim one—that Courtney and Jeff were waiting around for an opening.

But Brooke proved to be more realistic than Chase had given her credit for. At the Wedding of Your Dreams Chapel she motioned to him and they sat in one of the pews at the back of the traditional-themed room.

It was the sort of hearts-and-flowers place Chase pictured when he thought of weddings. He got the impression that Brooke was a hearts-and-flowers sort of woman.

She sat in the pew, her head back, eyes closed, exhaustion on her face.

For Chase, eloping was just a dumb move of Jeff's, but for Brooke it was so much more. From all she'd told him, she'd devoted herself to trying to make up for the financial loss she'd caused her parents and by association, her sister. For the past seven or so years, Brooke had worked to ensure that Courtney had a chance at college. And Courtney was throwing it all back in her face.

At least that was how Brooke saw it. As far as Chase was concerned, Brooke had succeeded. Courtney *had* the opportunity, whatever she decided to do with it.

It called for a celebration, to his way of thinking.

He leaned over and whispered to her. "I'll be back in a few minutes."

She nodded without opening her eyes.

Chase went out into the lobby area past at least two waiting wedding parties and flagged down a harried-looking woman.

"Yes?"

Chase pointed to a three-rose arrangement that one of the waiting brides carried. "I'd like to buy one of those."

"I'm sorry, it's been so busy today. You'll have to refresh my memory—does it come with your package?"

Chase shook his head. "I'm working à la carte here."

Frowning, the woman said, "I'll have to check the cooler to see what we've got available. We might be out of red roses. It's that time of year."

She looked around, then went into the back. Chase could hear her talking to someone, then she returned and beckoned to him. "Harry will help you."

Chase went into the back and saw a uniformed man staring into the cooler. "No red ro—"

"Harry!" The woman reentered the room carrying the three-rose arrangement Chase had noticed earlier. "She's changed her mind and wants a white nosegay. Can you do one in a hurry? We're running behind schedule."

Harry reached for a nosegay marked "reserved—

Howell" and plucked off the card. "Give her this one and I'll make another."

"You're a doll," said the woman and hurried out.

Chase whipped out his credit card. "I believe I'll take these."

Harry rang up his purchase. "Decided to bite the wedding bullet, huh?"

Chase smiled and said a noncommittal, "Thinking about it."

And with heart-stopping stunned surprise, he realized he *was*.

THIS WAS a hideous and horrible day, Brooke decided. Except for Chase. He hadn't been hideous and horrible. Except for the fact that she thought she might be in love with him. That wasn't hideous and horrible.

Except that it was. Love took time to nurture. This wasn't love—this was a hurricane, arriving with lots of energy and excitement, but blowing itself out shortly after, leaving destruction in its wake.

If she didn't watch herself, she was going to be left picking up the pieces.

She heard him return and sit next to her just as the taped organ music began. It occurred to her that she'd seen plenty of weddings today and the music had been different at each one.

Moments later, she felt something soft and velvety touch her lips. She smelled roses and opened her eyes. "Chase!" He held out three gorgeous red roses wrapped in a red-and-white ribbon with hearts and cupids printed on it.

"Happy Valentine's Day," he said softly.

Brooke buried her nose in one of the flowers so that he wouldn't see how touched she was. She'd never received roses for Valentine's Day before. She'd never happened to be dating anyone around that time of year.

"Thanks," she managed to say.

"They're also in celebration of your achievement."

"What achievement?"

"Wasn't your goal to give Courtney a chance at college?"

Brooke nodded.

"So, you did it."

"But—"

Chase shook his head. "You gave Courtney the *opportunity*. What she chooses to do with it is out of your hands."

"I never thought of it like that." But it was true. Courtney *could* go to college if she wanted to. Brooke stared at her roses. "You're a pretty smart guy."

"Shh!" A woman shushed them. "They're about to start!"

They sat through that wedding and two more, talking in between ceremonies. They watched as couple after couple kissed passionately and couple after couple left for their wedding night.

And Brooke snapped. *She* wanted to be one of those happy couples. Here she sat with a kind, decent, honorable man who was the best kisser she'd ever encountered, a man who could arouse her to the point of insanity, but had this commitment problem and, therefore, was not perfect. And his being not perfect made him...perfect.

The chapel minister approached and sat in the pew directly in front of them. "Having second thoughts?"

"What?" Brooke asked.

He smiled. "I've watched you two sitting here and talking. I think it's good that you're giving this some thought. Marriage is a serious business."

"Oh! We're not—I mean..." Brooke saw his gaze dip to her flowers and figured she'd better just stay quiet.

"Yes, marriage is a serious business. And it can be a scary business, but sometimes, you just have to take a leap of faith and trust that it's the right thing to do." He stood and put his hand on Chase's shoulder as he walked past.

"Why didn't you say anything?" Brooke asked.

Chase gave her a resigned look. "In a conversation like that, anything a man says will make him look like a jerk. He was talking to you, anyway. It's assumed that because I actually showed up, you're the one getting cold feet."

"In that case, it's time to leave."

"More chapels?"

Brooke shook her head. "Home."

They walked back to the parking lot, but their luck had run out there, as well. The car wouldn't start. Chase raised the hood, took one look, and shut it again. "The battery has boiled dry. The agency should have checked the water level before they let you drive off."

Brooke's shoulder's slumped. "I took the car without an inspection." At his chastising look, she added, "I was in a hurry."

"Let's go back to the chapel. Maybe we can hire the limo to take us to the airport."

Brooke had had enough of chapels and weddings and feeling sorry for herself, but there wasn't much choice.

As they walked, Chase threw his arm around her shoulder. "Everything's going to work out. We did our best."

Actually, Brooke felt better about having his arm around her shoulder than she did by what he said.

"I thought you'd be back," the minister said when he saw them. "I can tell you're crazy about each other. All you two needed was a little nudge." He clearly was going to take credit for doing the nudging.

Brooke hated to disillusion him. "Actually, all we need is the limo."

"The Love in the Limo package! We haven't done one of those yet today." He looked at his watch. "Hey, you're in luck. I've got a midnight wedding, but if we move fast I can work you two in, have the limo drop me back here and you'll be on your own."

"We just need to hire the limo to take us to the airport." Chase plucked a credit card from his wallet.

"No!" The man took the card. "You've come all

this way...you got a license, the flowers...it's Valentine's Day. And the limo special expires at midnight."

"License!" Brooke and Chase stared at each other.

"Don't tell me you two don't have a license."

"I should have checked there first," Brooke said. "I can't believe I've been such an idiot."

"Now, little lady, don't worry. We've got time. The bureau doesn't close until midnight. We'll just take the limo over there."

"But—"

Chase interrupted. "Sounds good. How much?"

"Marge?" the man called. "Since we're in a bit of a rush here, I'll get my equipment and Marge will take care of you."

Marge came out of the back room. "Love in the Limo," the minister said as he passed the woman the credit card.

"How much?" Chase repeated his question.

"Two hundred dollars. That includes the minister's gratuity, but not the driver's, two hours in our stretch limousine, the wedding ceremony, champagne and our Valentine Special." She reached into a basket by the desk and brought out a disposable wedding camera. "And you already have a three-rose upgrade, so I'll throw in a boutonniere."

"We don't—" Brooke began to object.

"That'll be fine." Chase handed Brooke the camera. "And add the driver's gratuity to the total, will you?"

"A taxi would be cheaper," Brooke muttered.

"I don't want to wait for a taxi." Chase looked down at her. "So I'm not."

Fine. Whatever. Brooke didn't want to argue. She suddenly wanted to drive around Las Vegas in a limo and drink cheap champagne. Why not? It was a cheap champagne kind of day.

The minister returned carrying a book and a boom box. "Do you have a musical preference?"

"No," Brooke said.

"Yes." Chase looked down at her, a whimsical curve to his lips. "Traditional all the way."

"Would that be traditional contemporary, or the classic traditional?"

"Classic," Chase answered.

"We need to hurry," Brooke reminded him.

The minister grinned as he popped a cassette into the boom box. "Once they make up their minds..." He laughed and slapped Chase's arm. "I'm Reverend Bob, by the way."

"I'm Chase and this is Brooke."

Reverend Bob laughed again. "As in she led you a merry chase, eh?"

The way Chase smiled, Brooke guessed that he'd had fun made of his name before. But then, so had she.

Reverend Bob led the way to a huge, white, stretched-to-the-max limo.

"Can that thing go around corners?" Brooke asked.

"Harry, here, is an expert."

"I thought Harry was the florist," Chase said.

"A man of many talents." Reverend Bob ushered them inside.

Brooke scooted to the far side of a padded bench seat. "It looks like a wedding threw up in here."

"Shh." Chase slid in beside her.

Reverend Bob sat across from them. On either side were garlands of greenery, flowers and ribbons.

"Since we have some time before we begin the ceremony, I'll just point out the special features of this particular limo." Reverend Bob gestured to the opaque glass partition behind him. "Soundproof. We'll lower it during the ceremony so Harry can be your witness, but once you begin your honeymoon, it'll be raised." He cleared his throat. "Some couples wanted it left down, but it's now our policy that it will be raised for the duration of the honeymoon."

"Honeymoon?" Brooke asked.

"Yes. You've got the limo for two hours." He gestured for them to move apart, reached between them and lowered a padded panel. "You pull that handle there, and the seat will fold down to make a bed."

Brooke was dumbfounded. He expected...people actually...

"Cool," was Chase's only comment.

"But...but..." Brooke gestured to the windows.

"They're tinted and you also have these." Reverend Bob pulled down a shade in a stained-glass pattern. "And the switch on the side opens the skylight."

"And when the time is right, you have your champagne." He indicated a recessed well filled with ice and a bottle of sparkling wine.

Reverend Bob pressed a button on the boom box and the strains of a familiar Bach piece filled the limo.

"Now, young lady, here is your groom's flower. I'll let you pin it on him. And son," the reverend gestured and finished with a whisper, "tighten the tie."

Chase obligingly tightened the knot on his tie and Brooke, feeling incredibly awkward, pinned a red rose to his lapel.

When were they going to tell the man that they weren't getting married?

Probably after they got to the license place. That was the important thing right now—that and getting to the airport. Brooke decided to just sit back and relax.

THE MUSIC was soothing, the ride was smooth and the sights were incredible. All in all, Chase thought, not a bad way to spend the twenty minutes it took to drive to the Clark County Marriage License Bureau on Third Street.

Reverend Bob pulled him aside. "You'll need thirty-five dollars, cash only."

"I've got it covered," Chase said.

He and Brooke hurried into the license place. Ten minutes later, they'd learned that there was no record of a Jeff Ryan and Courtney Weathers being issued a license. Chase took his first easy breath in hours.

Brooke just stared, first at the woman, then at Chase. "I can't believe it. We should have come here first. *I* should have come here first. What was I thinking? I have *completely* trashed this entire day, not only for you, but—"

"Will that be all, hon?" the woman at the counter asked in a disinterested voice.

"All? *All?*" Brooke gave a funny little laugh that sounded on the verge of hysteria. "What else could there be?"

"Brooke." Chase fought the urge to wrap his arms around her.

"I just can't get it right. I try." She looked at Chase, her eyes huge. "I try to get it right."

"So do I. Sometimes it...just...doesn't happen the..." He trailed off as he looked down at her. Brooke. He mentally trashed his life's timetable. Brooke. He removed the emotional barriers. Surrendered. Brooke. *Brooke.*

And an idea grew, probably from the seed planted at the wedding chapel. A wild idea. A crazy idea. An idea that made all the air leave his lungs. An idea that made his heart pound.

An idea that he knew was the best idea he'd ever had.

Brooke was oblivious to his idea. "I've been responsible, hardworking—and I've voted in every election. Not many people can say that." She turned to the woman at the counter. "Can you say that? Have you voted in every election?"

"Move along, hon. There's a line."

"*Brooke.*"

She shook off his arm. "Please check the computer again."

One look at Brooke and the woman knew it would be faster to do as she asked than argue.

"Brooke, I've got an idea."

"Just a *minute*, Chase." She stood on her toes so she could see the computer monitor.

Okay, then. Chase got out his wallet, counted out thirty-five dollars in cash and removed his driver's license. "Your wallet is in your purse, right?"

"Yeah." Without looking away from the computer, Brooke felt around in her shoulder bag and pulled out a black leather wallet.

Chase removed her driver's license. "You used to have curly hair," he commented, but Brooke ignored him.

"No Ryan, no Weathers," the woman said with stern finality.

Chase put down the thirty-five dollars and their driver's licenses and pushed them toward the woman. "We'll take a license."

Brooke stared blankly at him. "You aren't getting a license *for* them, are you?"

"No." He smiled. "I'm getting one for us."

She blinked. "You aren't serious."

"I am. Very serious."

"You're crazy."

"I am. Crazy for you."

"Oh, please. Now I know you're joking, because that is the *worst* line I've ever—"

He kissed her. It seemed like the right time, if not exactly the right place. As always, desire welled up within him. And he actually thought he could walk away from this.

He was never going to find this all-consuming passion with another woman and he wouldn't settle for less. Couldn't settle for less. Brooke was his and he was hers and it was time she realized it.

Except that she'd already realized it and that was why she'd been so cold with him. Cold when she wasn't kissing him, that is.

He loved the feel of her mouth beneath his. Loved the way they fit so perfectly, which boded well for other fittings.

There was the sound of a clearing throat. "Sign, please," the woman instructed them.

What was his name? Oh, yes. Chase scrawled an approximation of his signature and handed the pen to Brooke.

"But—"

"Sign." He kissed her again, quick and hard.

Brooke signed.

11

CHASE HAD TO GIVE Brooke two more reminder kisses between the door of the license bureau and the door of the limo.

Once they were back inside, Reverend Bob pulled the stained-glass shades, lit a fat white candle and opened his book. The music made a subtle shift. The lights dimmed and the fake candle-flame lightbulbs flickered in the wall sconces. "Would you place the rings on the book, please?"

Chase's blood went cold. He felt Brooke look at him, but he couldn't meet her eyes.

"So we're not quite ready. Not a problem." Reverend Bob punched the stop button, closed his book and picked up what Chase had thought was another book. He unzipped the cover and opened it to reveal a velvet-lined ring case stocked with plain gold and silver wedding bands. He eyed Brooke. "Gold or silver?"

"Gold," she whispered.

Reverend Bob gave her two to try on. "Single-or double-ring ceremony?"

"Double," Brooke said firmly and Chase started trying on the plain gold bands.

Reverend Bob coughed a discreet, "One-fifty."

"Plastic?"

"Naturally."

Chase handed him his credit card. It seemed like a good time to kiss Brooke again, so he did, stopping only when the music began. He didn't need the reassurance—it was for Brooke. Oddly, for someone who had carefully planned and considered each move he made, Chase had never felt such absolute confidence that he was doing the right thing.

"Place your rings on the book."

They did so.

Holding their license out to the side, Reverend Bob began. "Do you, Chase Michael Davenport, take Brooke...Lynn?"

The breath hissed between Brooke's teeth. "Yes, Brooke Lynn like the bridge. Ha ha. Please continue."

"Take Brooke Lynn Weathers as your lawfully wedded wife?"

"I do," Chase said, trying to put as much meaning into the words as he could.

"Will you honor her, cherish and keep her, in sickness and in health, for richer or for poorer, forsaking all others, keeping yourself only unto her as long as you both shall live?"

"I will."

Reverend Bob turned to Brooke and repeated the questions. She must have answered, but Chase couldn't tell because a buzzing had started in his head and continued as they exchanged the gold rings. He was pretty sure it was happiness—or maybe the realization that he was minutes away from a genuine honeymoon.

"Do you two wish to express vows of your own?"

Chase looked at her and said with all the eloquence he could muster, "Brooke...we're doing the right thing."

She gazed back and responded with equal eloquence. "I sincerely hope so."

They nodded at Reverend Bob, who smiled beatifically. "By the authority invested in me by the state of Nevada, I pronounce you husband and wife. You may now kiss...but I see you already know this part."

AS HE LEFT the limo, Reverend Bob handed Chase an envelope. "My personal wedding gift to you. Have a long life and have fun living it."

Chase's fingers immediately identified the familiar outline of a condom. "Thanks!" he called after Reverend Bob. "And I mean that."

The Reverend saluted him and went inside the chapel.

Now all Chase had to do was figure out how to suggest to his new bride that they unfold the seat.

He raised the window to discover that Brooke had already closed the partition, had removed the padded panel and was tugging at the seat.

"Harry will take us to the airport. Ten minutes before our time is up, music starts playing." She flipped the switch on the side and the ceiling slid to the back, exposing a window open to the sky. "Oh! Look at the stars. They're beautiful and I want you to see them now, because you're not going to have time later."

"Brooke?" Chase took hold of the pull handle. "I love you."

Brooke grinned. "But how well do you love, that's the question. And I want it answered. Now."

Chase yanked the seat and it unfolded and clicked into place revealing a white satin sheet-covered bed with two heart-shaped pillows and a note.

The note contained discreet instructions for access to the contents of the compartment opposite the champagne bucket.

Chase turned the knob and discovered toiletries packets. "All the comforts of home."

"And more." Brooke spread her hand over the sheets. "I've always wondered what satin sheets would be like."

They stared at the bed, then at each other.

For Chase, the first time with a woman was a slow, thorough and deliberate exploration. He liked it that way. He looked forward to the gradual building and release of passion.

With Brooke, there was an explosion.

The insanity that had gripped them first in his office, and then each time they touched, took over.

He reached for her, she reached for him and they tumbled sideways onto the bed, kissing frantically, grabbing for buttons, unzipping zippers and ripping off clothes.

All Chase could think about—when he thought at all—was that he didn't have to fight this obsession with Brooke anymore. He could give in to it, revel in it, celebrate it. And Brooke could do the same.

And she was doing very well at the celebrating part, since she was now on top of him.

Brooke pressed dozens of kisses over any area she could reach and since they were both naked, she could reach a lot. And did.

He ran his hands over her back, curving around her hips and as far down her thighs as he could reach, savoring the feel of her body against his at last. Then he plunged his fingers into her hair and brought her mouth to meet his.

Ah, yes. Passion, desire, lust, or some nameless emotion that transcended all three, built until he could barely tolerate it and still remain conscious. The feeling was so strong, it was almost tangible.

Chase understood how men could betray countries, start wars or pawn their honor for women who made them feel this way.

"It's not enough," Brooke moaned against his mouth. "I'm on fire, but I'm not hot enough...."

Chase wasn't even aware of moving, but now he realized that Brooke, soft, warm and insistently passionate Brooke, was beneath him and that he had access to all sorts of soft, warm and passionate places that he'd had trouble reaching before.

He reached them now, with his mouth, his tongue and his fingers, guided by Brooke's feverishly whispered demands.

"More!"

"Faster!"

"Here!"

And then, "Now!"

He rocked into her, plunging deeply and gasping at the incredible wonder of it all.

"Chase...please?" It was a softly worded plea, different from the others and all the more erotic because of it.

Brooke wrapped her legs around his waist as he continued rocking, the rhythm and vibrations of the limo complementing each thrust.

And then the vibrations came from within Brooke as she buried her face in his shoulder and moaned her pleasure.

Hearing her, feeling her arms and legs tighten around him, triggered his own powerful release. A thundering roar filled his head and drowned out his shouts.

They lay together just breathing. All Chase's muscles quivered with the aftermath.

And yet he'd have to possess her again soon. Already he could feel the tension building, as though it were a low rumble growing ever louder until it drowned out all thought and sound.

Brooke sighed. "We must be near the airport. I can hear the planes."

Chase rolled to the side and hauled her next to him. They looked at the stars in the black sky above them, until they faded with the approach of the airport lights.

A moment later, soft music filled the limo. Chase gave Brooke one last kiss.

She smiled up at him. "I do love you. I tried not to, but—"

"I'm irresistible?"

"I couldn't help it."

"Guess what? Now you don't have to."

IF THEY'D BEEN ABLE to return to Houston on the same plane, their lives might have been different, but since Chase's car was in San Antonio and Brooke's was in Houston, they ended up on different flights.

For the first hour or so, Brooke relived every moment of her spontaneous wedding and honeymoon. But sometime during the second hour, it became less and less real and more and more, what-have-I-done?

She was married. To a man she'd known barely two weeks. She felt she'd known him longer, she felt as though she was in love with him, but she couldn't be. This wasn't the way people fell in love—at least not the happily-ever-after kind of love. This was nothing but a physical attraction. There was no foundation to support it. One argument, one crisis, and it would collapse.

They hadn't discussed what would happen next. Would he move in with her? Should she move in with him? What about Jeff? What about Courtney?

Brooke buried her face in her hands. Courtney. How could she face Courtney? How could Brooke tell her sister she'd just up and married someone she barely knew all because of the way he made her feel?

Hadn't she always told Courtney not to let her

emotions run away with her? To think things through?

And...and her wedding. She'd gotten married in a vulgar limousine and then had sex while being driven around by a stranger who knew exactly what they were doing.

No church, no white dress to pass down to her daughter, no something borrowed, something blue, no wedding cake—they hadn't even had time for the champagne.

Brooke felt sick to her stomach. What had happened to her?

And what was going to happen next?

By the time Brooke walked into her house, it was a quarter to five and she didn't feel like sleeping. She didn't know what she felt like doing. She walked up the stairs, very calmly, turned down the hallway, also very calmly, and opened the door to Courtney's bedroom to find her sister asleep in her bed. Very calmly.

She then went back downstairs and made herself a can of chicken noodle soup because it seemed like a good thing to eat at 5:00 a.m. after a day of chasing her sister all over Las Vegas, then getting married and having a glorious, earth shattering time in the back of a limo.

All in all, it hadn't been one of her typical Valentine's Days.

She wasn't trying to wake up Courtney, but she wasn't trying to be particularly quiet, either.

She was slurping her second bowl of soup when Courtney shuffled into the kitchen.

"*Where* have you been?" she asked, arms crossed over her chest.

"Looking for you," Brooke told her—calmly.

"You could have called, or left me a note—I was worried!"

Brooke chased the last of the noodles around her bowl. "Now you know how I felt when I got the call from the school yesterday. I couldn't find you anywhere and discovered that there had been no play rehearsal before school and that Jeff was also absent."

"Well, I—"

"I called *hospitals*, Courtney."

Looking miserable, Courtney slumped into the chair opposite Brooke.

Brooke wished she didn't look miserable, not because she didn't want Courtney feeling bad, but because she wasn't finished ranting yet. She'd barely started. She hadn't even managed a good yell.

"We cut school," Courtney mumbled.

"Yes. To go to Las Vegas and get married."

Courtney's head shot up. "How did you know—"

"When I couldn't find you, I searched your room. I found all the little clues you left." Brooke carried the bowl over to the sink and rinsed it out. "Just as you wanted me to, isn't that right, Courtney?"

"You searched my room?"

It was a nice touch, the surprised outrage. Brooke told her so.

Her sister gave her a wary look.

"You never intended to go to Las Vegas. You just wanted me to think that's where you went. And you did a fabulous job. So fabulous that both Chase and I ended up there."

Courtney gasped.

"You deserve applause." Brooke clapped her hands. "Actresses crave applause, don't they Courtney?"

"Brooke, I don't know what you're talking about."

Brooke shook her head in wonder. "You're quite an actress. It would be a shame to waste talent like that, so go ahead. Do what you want with your life."

"What do you mean?"

"I mean go to school where you want, or don't go to school. Get married, or don't get married. It's up to you. Me, I'm going to bed."

CHASE STOOD OVER Jeff's sleeping body and roughly shook his shoulder.

"Mmm."

"Jeff!"

"Whu...oh, Chase. Hey, man. Where've you been?"

"Las Vegas."

"I thought you were going to San Antonio."

"I did." Chase nudged Jeff over with his foot, then sat on the edge of the bed. "And then I went to Las Vegas, where I spent hours looking for you and your girlfriend. Then I flew back to San Antonio and drove three hours to Houston. It is now dawn. Dawn is a great time of day. Things become very clear at dawn."

Jeff blinked at him. "You *went* to Las Vegas?"

"Yes."

"Man." Jeff sat up and rubbed his eyes. "You weren't supposed to actually *go* there."

"Just to think that *you* had."

"Yeah," Jeff admitted, then winced. "Oh, *man*."

"So this was a set up."

Jeff slumped dejectedly. "Yeah."

"How much?"

"All of it," he admitted reluctantly.

"The marriage part?" At least they weren't engaged.

Exhaling, Jeff mumbled. "Everything. Courtney and I aren't even dating. We're just friends."

Chase felt numb, mainly because his emotions were all worn out. But Brooke—when she found out... "So why the act?"

"It was Courtney's idea—"

"I should have guessed.

"Hey, don't blame her. I went along with it. All we wanted to do was to stop you and her sister from interfering in our lives."

"If you handled your life better, you wouldn't need interference, as you call it."

"Look. I don't want to go to college, study business and end up like you—no offense. But you won't listen."

"I'm listening now."

"Well, the thing is, I didn't really want to go anywhere. But I've been hanging around Courtney and working on the play, and I've figured out that I'm good at that stuff. I like the special effects that I've been doing on the computer. I programed all the lighting and, man, there's so much out there to learn. I found out that the University of Northern Los Angeles has a great program. And...and so I applied."

Chase was completely floored. "Have you heard anything yet?"

Jeff shook his head. "Mid-March if I'm accepted, then there will be a big deposit due. I'm kinda hoping you'll okay it."

All Chase had wanted was for Jeff to have a focus. Now, it appeared that he did. "If that's what you want to do, then I'll recommend it to your mom."

"Thanks and, uh, sorry you made that trip for nothing. Are you real mad?"

"It wasn't for nothing and I'm too tired to be mad." Chase stood. "It's almost time for you to get up. Get dressed now, and maybe you'll have time for breakfast for once."

AFTER JEFF LEFT for school, Chase sat in the kitchen drinking coffee, when he should have been sleeping. But he didn't feel like sleeping. He felt like trying to figure out what on earth he'd done.

He was no better than his father, who'd fallen for Jeff's beautiful and flaky mother. That had been an impulsive marriage, and look what had happened.

Not that Brooke was in any way like Zoe, but...Chase drained the last of his coffee and decided to do something he should have done long ago—visit his father.

YEARS AGO, Albert Davenport had left his field sales job—about the time he'd married Zoe, actually—and had moved into management.

When Chase knocked on his office door, his father was on the telephone. One look at Chase and he finished the call.

"Well, Chase. Long time no see."

"I know." Chase moved some files off the only chair in the office and sat down. "I've come to apologize."

"Ahh."

"I wasn't very nice to you about Zoe."

"No, you weren't."

So his father wasn't going to make it easy for him. Chase was too tired and too confused to care. "I never understood how you could be taken in by a woman like that—"

"Wait a minute. I wasn't taken in by her. I knew exactly who and what she was and I don't regret a minute of our marriage."

"You don't?"

"Not a bit." His father studied him. "Every man needs a Zoe in his life at least once to remind him that life is good and he's still a man. Suppose you tell me about your Zoe."

How had he known? Chase shifted uncomfortably. "Brooke isn't a Zoe."

"Tell me about your Brooke, then."

"When I'm around her, I..." He spread his hands. This was his father, after all.

"Can't think of anything else?"

"No."

Albert smiled and got a faraway look in his eyes. "My best advice is to hang on and enjoy the ride."

"Well, that's the problem. I think it's going to be a short one."

BROOKE HAD LEFT a message for Chase and then had worried herself silly waiting for him to call back. When the phone rang, she nearly jumped out of her skin.

"Hey," he said softly.

Brooke swallowed and said what had to be said. "Chase, we need to talk."

"Yeah, there are some details we need to work out, but I have a feeling that's not what you mean."

No, it wasn't. She couldn't believe they were married. Couldn't believe she'd been so rash. Couldn't believe that what she felt for him was an everlasting love. It just didn't happen that fast. She wanted reassurance. She needed reassurance. She needed him.

"I've been thinking. It's just...I mean we didn't think about the details, the living arrangements and all those things we brought up with Courtney and Jeff."

"We can work it out." He sounded so stoic.

Something squeezed Brooke's heart and wouldn't let go.

He regretted what he'd done. She knew it with every fiber of her being and every fiber of her being didn't want him to say the words.

So, she said them instead. "I think we've made a mistake."

"Oh, wow, Jeff. Character Psychology class is awesome. I think I know what happened with Chase and Brooke."

"I know *something* happened in Vegas, but they never said. And Chase has been driving me nuts for months now with the calls and the e-mails."

"Oh, I know. But you know what? I don't think they hate each other at all. I think they've got a thing for each other."

"Then why don't they get together and leave us alone?"

"Because they're both stubborn. They need to be locked in a room somewhere until they work out whatever it is."

"Hey—I'm willing to try anything at this point."

"I can't believe you invited Jeff and Chase and Chase's father for Thanksgiving dinner." Brooke peeled potatoes and watched as Courtney concocted some strange vegetable dish.

"So you've said at least once every fifteen minutes. What you haven't said is why it bothers you."

And Brooke wasn't going to. She and Chase had quietly and legally disentangled themselves and she'd found that it was more painful than she would have believed.

She couldn't get over him. Her...*thing* for him should have burnt itself out long ago, but it seemed just as strong as ever. Seeing him again after so many months...well, knowing what she was capable of made Brooke nervous.

"It doesn't *bother* me," she said. "But I've always thought of Thanksgiving as family time."

"Yeah, me, too." Courtney turned to her. "But it's a lot of trouble to go to just for the two of us."

"I don't mind," Brooke said.

"What happened in Las Vegas?"

Brooke dropped the potato peeler. "I should rinse this off." Talk about out of the blue.

But her sister was persistent. "What happened between you and Chase in Las Vegas?"

"Nothing." Brooke ran hot water over the peeler, then resumed her chore.

"Something happened. You've been acting weird ever since you got back. And according to Jeff, so has Chase."

How was she going to bluff her way out of this? "Well, I guess it's because we...jumped to conclusions. We let our emotions run away with us. I can't speak for Chase, but it also showed me just how far I was willing to go to try to influence you. I mean, I just walked away from my job. I had an interview scheduled and I let the poor girl show up and wait until somebody told her I wasn't there. Ever since," Brooke swallowed, then went on, "Ever since I was your age, I've thought of myself as levelheaded and in control. This showed me I wasn't."

"And that's what you've been upset about ever since February? I don't think so."

"Drop it, Courtney."

"I can't. Jeff and I are taking a psychology and characterization class and we've learned some fascinating behavioral theories. Really great stuff for getting into the meat of a character. Stuff I wouldn't have learned in straight film school, so you were right about college."

Brooke managed a smile.

"Okay, now I know something's up because no human could have resisted gloating after all the trouble I gave you about going to college."

"Are you going to need the microwave soon, or can I cook the potatoes now?" Brooke added water to the dish and put on the lid.

"You had a fling with Chase, didn't you?"

Brooke shoved the dish into the microwave, set it for ten minutes and punched start.

"I'm right, aren't I?" Courtney raised her arms in a victory salute. "I knew it! You had a fling and now you're embarrassed to face him. I don't know why you're ashamed of it. He's a great guy and Jeff and I always thought you two would be good together. In fact that was our original plan—to set you up. We just didn't realize that it worked."

"It didn't work."

"Why not?"

"We...we rushed into...things and...it just didn't work out, so leave it, okay?" Brooke glared at Courtney. "Hurry up with the vegetables."

As it turned out, Brooke realized she'd worried too

much. Chase was excruciatingly polite and avoided looking at her.

Brooke was equally polite and a faultless hostess.

Thanksgiving dinner was a splendid feast with traditional foods and no cooking failures. It should have been a perfect day.

And Brooke was miserable.

"More coffee anyone?" Courtney chirped.

Albert Davenport accepted a cup, then said, "I'll just take mine in the den and watch the game. Anyone going to join me?"

"Sure, I'll—" Jeff broke off abruptly. "I'll catch up with you."

Courtney waited until Albert had left the dining room and then announced, "Chase, Brooke—Jeff and I have something to show you."

An ominous prickle started at the base of Brooke's spine. She shot a look at Chase to find him regarding her with equal concern. They followed Courtney back to the spare bedroom. Courtney stopped at the doorway and ushered Brooke and Chase inside.

"What?" Brooke asked.

"You two are bugging us," Jeff said. "The constant e-mails, the phone calls—we can't stand it."

"Now, something happened between you in Las Vegas and you still haven't worked it out." Courtney started to shut the door. "So you're going to stay in here until you do." With that, she shut the door.

"And they accuse *us* of interfering," Chase muttered.

"This is ridiculous." Brooke pushed open the door

to find Jeff moving a chest of drawers in front of it. "Hey!"

"We mean it," Courtney's voice came from behind the dresser.

"We could knock this over," Brooke threatened.

"Not when we get through with barricading you inside. We've had lots of practice in the dorm."

"Court—"

Chase interrupted her with a simple touch to her arm. And then a touch to her other arm. And then he shut the door.

"Have you been as miserable as I have?" His face was open and vulnerable.

"At least."

"What do you want to do?"

"I know what I want to do," Brooke said. "But what do you want to do?"

His gaze held hers. "I want to do it over again. I want to go back to when we got on separate planes and get on the same one to San Antonio. And then I would have driven you to the airport in Houston to get your car. And we would have talked our way into a real marriage." He took a step toward her. "Because that's what we had and we just didn't know it."

Tears rolled down Brooke's cheeks. "But we didn't."

"And *that* was the only mistake we made!" He looked fierce and possessive. "Except for the one where I let you talk yourself into a divorce."

"You didn't argue very hard."

"Pride," he said simply. "I've missed you."

Warmth began creeping through her. It felt so good. "You've missed this." She knew he was feeling it, too.

"I've missed you *and* I've missed this."

His mouth captured hers and once more, Brooke was drawn into the maelstrom of sensation. Time hadn't diminished her reaction. If anything, it had strengthened it. They tumbled to the bed, shedding their clothes in an attempt to get as close as possible to each other.

Brooke knew nothing would satisfy her until they were joined together once more.

"I need you, Brooke." Chase spoke in a fierce whisper, his gaze locked on her.

"Need, oh, yes. Please."

In contrast to the way it had been before, Chase eased into her and stopped, searching her eyes.

"What?" Her voice sounded irritable, even to her. And completely justified, she might add.

"Think. Is this what you want?"

"How can you ask that?" Wasn't he burning up with the wanting?

He smiled, but she felt his arms quiver with the effort of holding back. "You've been afraid of giving in to your emotions, so this time, let your head decide."

She knew what he was saying, and appreciated it, really she did. But his timing was really bad. "It's lasted, hasn't it? You and me."

"Yeah."

"You think we made a mistake."

"Not about this," he said. "And speaking of thinking, could you do it a little faster?"

"We messed up our marriage."

"We can fix it...Brooke?"

"What about you—why didn't you try to talk me out of the divorce?"

"Leftover baggage from my dad. Can we discuss the details later?"

"But you said—"

"I've changed my mind!" He began to move.

"About me?"

"Hmm?"

"You've changed your mind about me?"

He mumbled something that sounded like "no," but Brooke stopped caring when he kissed her and maneuvered his hand between them.

"Ooo, Chhaaaassssee . . ."

"That's what I like to hear," he gasped before burying himself deep within her.

Afterwards, Chase raised himself on an elbow. "Who knew your head was such a talker?"

"Yeah." Brooke smiled. "So now what do we do?"

"Jeff, help me get this table on top of the dresser."

"Gee, Courtney, are you sure that's enough? You've got half the furniture in your house in the hall."

Still arguing, their voices receded.

"You know," Chase said. "When we get out, we're going to Las Vegas."

"I know," Brooke replied.

"I want to take another limo ride."

"You think we can book it for four hours this time?"

"We can try." He dropped a kiss on her forehead, then another, then one on her nose and finally a long, lingering one on her lips. "But in the meantime, it seems a shame to make Jeff and Courtney move the furniture after they just finished trapping us in here. What do you think?"

Brooke reached for him. "My head says go for it."

And they did.

Pamela Burford presents

The Wedding Ring

Four high school friends and a pact—
every girl gets her ideal mate by thirty or be
prepared for matchmaking! The rules are
simple. Give your "chosen" man three
months...and see what happens!

Love's Funny That Way
Temptation #812—on sale December 2000
It's no joke when Raven Muldoon falls in love with comedy
club owner Hunter—*brother* of her "intended."

I Do, But Here's the Catch
Temptation #816—on sale January 2001
Charli Ross is more than willing to give up her status as
last of a dying breed—the thirty-year-old virgin—to Grant.
But all *he* wants is marriage.

One Eager Bride To Go
Temptation #820—on sale February 2001
Sunny Bleecker is still waiting tables at Wafflemania when
Kirk comes home from California and wants to marry her.
It's as if all her dreams have finally come true—except...

Fiancé for Hire
Temptation #824—on sale March 2001
No way is Amanda Coppersmith going to let
The Wedding Ring rope her into marriage. But no matter
how clever she is, Nick is one step ahead of her...

"Pamela Burford creates the
memorable characters readers love!"
—The Literary Times

#1 *New York Times* bestselling author

NORA ROBERTS

brings you more of the loyal and loving,
tempestuous and tantalizing Stanislaski family.

Coming in February 2001

The Stanislaski Sisters
Natasha and Rachel

Though raised in the Old World traditions of their
family, fiery Natasha Stanislaski and cool, classy
Rachel Stanislaski are ready for a *new* world of love....

*And also available in February 2001 from
Silhouette Special Edition, the newest book in the
heartwarming Stanislaski saga*

CONSIDERING KATE

Natasha and Spencer Kimball's daughter Kate turns her
back on old dreams and returns to her hometown, where
she finds the *man* of her dreams.

Available at your favorite retail outlet.

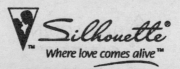

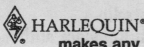